MURDER AT THE PINK PRISON

Much love
Happy Birthday!
Terry

Murder at the Pink Prison
©2015 Terry Ward

This is a work of fiction. Resemblance to any person living or dead is purely coincidental.

"Emma" photograph by Tom Ward III ©2015

Dedicated, as always, to God, and also to my Mom

CHAPTER ONE

Nick DiPaulo hated hospitals. They gave him the creeps. His Florsheims snapped sharply against the marbled green tiles but it was as if he was invisible. The nurses carried on with what they were doing, cold, impersonal, efficient, not part of the human frailty that surrounded them. The real problem was that this scared the hell out of him. The big "C". He'd never actually known anyone who'd had it. But he knew what it meant. Cancer meant death. Long, painful, agonizing death. And just being here made him feel like he might get it too. He turned the corner and read the numbers on the doors as he passed. Three twelve...three fourteen...three sixteen. He took a deep breath then gave a sharp rap and stepped in.

One look at Moriarty told him he should've stayed away. It didn't even look like him. The brusque, burly director had shriveled to nothing and all he could think of was the day Moriarty had shoveled down one of Ralph's Reuben's. The sick man's florid complexion was now pale grey and his teeth pushed the skin of his chin forward awkwardly like a native's shrunken head. Nick felt like throwing up. His friend's eyes were closed and for a second he thought he might be able to slink away unnoticed, but no such luck.

Moriarty squinted an eye open and even with the faded grin, Nick saw the pain. "Look like shit, don't I."

His voice was hoarse, like sandpaper grating a rough piece of wood. Nick inwardly flinched.

"Yeah."

He reached for his pack of Lucky's, put one in his mouth and offered one to his friend.

Moriarty waved it away. "Asshole doctors won't let me."

"What do they know." He lit up and took a deep drag. He needed that.

"How ya feeling? Shit, Moriarty, they got you trussed up like a turkey."

Moriarty tried to pull himself up, his bony knuckles white with effort against the sterile sheets, then slid down once again. Nick looked under the bed and fumbled for the crank.

"Here. That high enough?"

"Yeah. That's good." Moriarty leaned his head back against the pillows and grimaced. He noticed the look on Nick's face. "Only four more treatments. It'll be okay. I'll be back before you get my seat warm."

Nick crushed out the cigarette and took a seat. He looked down at his hands. It was too hard to look at his friend.

"Spill it," Moriarty rasped.

"I'm not taking your place, Jim."

"Still got a bug up your ass, don't you. Give me a drink of water."

Nick poured some from the pitcher. It was lukewarm. He started to get up. "I'm gonna get some cold..."

Jim reached out for the glass. "Don't bother. Probably won't keep it down anyway."

He gave it over and Moriarty took a tiny sip, delicate, like a girl. He swallowed hard. This was the guy who drained a can of Schlitz like it was nothing, wiped his mouth. laughed and let out a huge belch as he asked for another. He had to stop these images running though his head.

"No bug, just don't want to get too..."

"Noticeable?" Moriarty gave a little laugh. "Afraid Samuels is gonna shove his nose up your butt again?"

"Nice image," he chuckled. "But, no, I don't give a shit about Ben Samuels. Truth is, I'm putting in my notice. One of the reasons I came today."

"You coulda just told Johnson."

He heard the tone in Moriarty's voice and it made him feel guilty. He was letting the guy down.

"You're my boss."

Moriarty closed his eyes and leaned his head back. "Yeah. I'm the boss. Some boss."

"You'll be back soon," Nick paused and looked down at his hands again. "Yeah..." The word drifted into the air between them and stayed. A big lie and they both knew it. Chances were he wouldn't make it all the way through the chemo. Even if he did, the cancer would probably win in the end, taking over his body until the guy was just screaming to die.

He got up and rubbed the back of his neck. There wasn't much for the two of them to say at this point. When Samuels had tried to fire him, Jim had gone toe-to-toe with the FBI Director of Operations and finagled a desk job for him. Now he was throwing it in his face, backing away from a dying friend's request like a coward. It wasn't just the thought of taking Moriarty's place that haunted him. There were other things, other people, he was backing away from too.

As if sensing the direction of his thoughts, Moriarty broke in. "You were stupid with that broad. What was her name?"

"Jill." Just her name on his tongue made him feel something he didn't like feeling. Like losing something really good that you knew you were never going to have again.

"That kind always goes for the money," Moriarty continued.

"Yeah."

Moriarty opened his eyes again. He looked so exhausted, so old, like death had already invaded him. "So what are you gonna do with yourself now, hotshot?"

He put his hands in his pockets and paced over by the window. "I'm gonna go into the bank with my old man. He finally got me, let's see if he still thinks it's such a great idea."

Moriarty gave a broken, barely audible chuckle. "You never stop wantin' to stick it to him, do ya, kid?" He waved his hand. "Don't matter. All kids want to do that to their old man. I wish ya luck. Shit, you'll be sittin' on a pile of dough in no time."

"I'll be sitting at a desk wishing Ed Bently hadn't missed when he tried to shoot me."

"Yeah, I know. And you're too stubborn to take what I'm offerin ya."

"It isn't that, Jim."

"Then what is it?"

"I think I just realized that I couldn't beat Samuels. In the end, he's going to win, and then what have I got? Thirty years sitting behind a desk waiting for the chance to get back in the field? You know, I had a vision of myself. I was fifty, Johnson's age, and the only thing I looked forward to was Friday nights when I'd sit my ass down at a bar and not have to get up the next morning for work. That's it. It's not for me, Jim. If I can't do what I wanted to do, I might as well be sitting on that pile of dough."

"You're stupid."

Moriarty was staring full on at him and there was disgust in his eyes.

"Yeah, maybe."

"I liked you, kid. I thought you were a dirty fighter and I liked that. We need more of that in the agency. Too many of these buttoned-down college boys who do everything by the book. I thought you were different. You're just a...," Moriarty tsked and began to get out of bed. "Help me get to the john."

He put his arm under Moriarty's and was shocked at how light the guy was. He was dying, but still fighting. And now he understood. Maybe he was running away from a fight.

Moriarty did his business and Nick helped him back into bed.

"You can't fight guys like Samuels, Moriarty. You know that. Look where it got you."

A laugh crackled out of what was left of Moriarty's lungs again. "Shows what you know, smart-ass. I got Samuels by the balls. I got stuff on him that'll never see the light of day, because he'll never want it to. That's what you do with guys like Samuels. You get dirtier than they are."

Moriarty took on a whole different light.

"Then why...?"

"Why didn't I climb the ladder? Why didn't I go further? Because I got right where I wanted to be and nobody's going to take that away from me. Why do you think I want you in my chair while I'm going through this shit?"

"Because I'm obviously the best you've got," he said sarcastically.

"Yeah. You are. But that's not why. I can trust you. You aren't going to stab me in the back. When I get back on my feet, there's not going to be any shit about me taking my spot back."

"You know I wouldn't."

"Yeah, I do. Besides, I know the truth about what happened that night with Cassetti. I know you lied through your teeth and Cassetti was the one that shot Bently."

Nick's mouth dropped open then he closed it.

"A little surprised, college boy? Think I don't know when somebody's feeding me a line of bullshit a mile wide? You covered up for a mafia boss in a murder investigation. That makes you an accessory after the fact and about a dozen other charges that would put you away in a federal pen for about thirty years. Cross me and I'll play you just like I play Samuels. You see, kid, I am a dirty fighter."

Instead of being offended, Moriarty went up a notch on his respect-o-meter. Yeah, he was a dirty fighter and Nick liked that. They understood each other. He felt the blood pumping through his veins in a way that he hadn't felt since that last night with Jill.

"So why don't you blackmail me into taking your spot?" He'd play along.

"You and I both know that ain't how it works."

Nick nodded. Already the idea of going into his father's bank was beginning to fade. Moriarty was offering him a life rope.

"I ain't dying, kid, if that's what you're thinkin'. I'm taking that spot back and you better be ready when I do."

Nick stood silent for a moment.

"I go back in the field afterwards?"

"I'll see what I can arrange."

"And when Samuels finds out I'm not sitting at a desk anymore?"

"You let me worry about him."

Maybe Moriarty was right. If anyone could beat cancer, he probably could.

He turned his collar up as he walked out to the car. Snowflakes swirled in the air. The guys at the office had kidded him about Binghamton in winter but it turned out that it was no joke. Only the beginning of November and he was already freezing his ass off. Almost made him wish he'd taken up his mother's offer about joining them in Bermuda over the holidays. Yeah, almost, but not quite. Barricaded in a bungalow with his father for two weeks was his idea of hell. He shivered. Yeah, and now he was going to have to explain why he wasn't coming into the bank after all. That oughta be a real laugh.

He unlocked his door and slid in. Cold air blasted from the vent and he turned off the heater while the car warmed up.

"...Record turnouts at voting booths. Exit polls don't favor either candidate. It's going to be close, folks..."

He turned the radio to the jazz station. Kennedy was going to win. Tricky Dick just looked too shifty. Should've never done that debate. Kennedy looked like a movie star next to him and a lot of women were voting. His mouth turned up on one side. He bet his mother had voted for Kennedy. She'd like it that he was Catholic. Wouldn't that piss his father off? Billie Holliday crooned to him over the air waves and he turned the heater back on then shoved the car into gear. It was three-thirty. Should be enough time.

Downtown was congested. Must've been early Christmas shoppers, maybe a few early election celebrations, some Democrats feeling up waitresses' asses as they downed their lunchtime martinis. He saw someone pull out of a parking spot and the taillights of the car just ahead of him came on but it was too late. He nosed his MG up the woman's butt giving her no room to back up and take the spot. She turned around and gave him a dirty look which he ignored.

"Go on, sweetheart. You got more time to shop than I do."

The woman went on and he took the spot. He locked the door and walked down the block to Drazen's. It was his mother's birthday that weekend and he was expected to drive down to DC for dinner. He grimaced. His father would probably ruin the whole thing when he gave him the big news. There weren't many things in this world that bothered his conscience, but causing his mother more pain than she already went through with the old man was one of them. And on her birthday. Nice one, DiPaulo. Great guy. Happy birthday, Mom.

A woman with bright red lipstick who'd probably been there for twenty years approached him. "Can I help you, sir?"

"Perfumes?" he asked.

"This way," she walked gracefully, like a model in an old movie, and then waved a hand towards a long counter. "Right over there, sir. I'm sure Janine will be able to help you."

"Thanks."

He walked over to the waiting Janine. She looked like she belonged behind a perfume counter, blonde and vague, with a sort of dreamy smile.

"Hello," she said. "Can I help you?"

"I'm looking for something for my mother. It's her birthday."

"I see." She selected a few bottles and one at a time held them out for him to smell.

"That's nice," he said. "What is it?"

"Chanel No. 5. It's a very sophisticated scent. I'm sure your mother would love it."

Sophisticated. He thought of his mother in her sedate gray sweater and pearls. Yeah. That was his mother. He grinned. "Probably. What's this one?"

She held the elegant bottle up. "Ah, Shalimar. Exotic."

It was like a sledgehammer hit him. The smell of it didn't conjure up images of his mother. Instead, it brought memories of a hot summer night, long tan legs, and green eyes that held a barrier between them even in bed. He felt parts of him tighten that had no business tightening there in the middle of a department store.

"I think we'll go with the other one." He forced thoughts of Jill out of his head.

"Very nice, sir. I'm sure your mother will love it."

"Can you gift wrap it?"

"Of course. If you'd like to wait a few minutes, I'll be right back."

"Sure."

She started to go and he stopped her. "Uh, fur scarves? Where are they?"

Her smiled deepened. He could almost read her thoughts, *"What a good son."* Not if you read my thoughts, honey.

"Third floor, sir. I'll have your package ready when you get back."

The elevator operator landed him on the third floor and he stepped into a different level of luxury. He looked around and saw the furs to the right. It wasn't Saks or Bergdorf's but for a small city, it wasn't bad. Looked like a pretty impressive array. He went over to a counter.

"Fur scarves?"

The saleswoman went off to find some samples. He turned and leaned against the counter, looking over into the round showroom surrounded by tall mirrors. A couple of salespeople hovered around a customer. His eyes perused the woman trying on a fur. Her honey colored hair was done up in a French twist and the fur she'd been trying on slid from her shoulders like a woman undressing for her lover. There was only one woman he knew that could do that. Jill.

A lot of questions flew around his head and before they had a chance to get answered she turned and their eyes met. Her mouth, that slightly full, beautiful mouth, opened slightly and her eyes widened, then she turned back around, ignoring him. A salesman helped her on with another coat. A white mink. It suited her and all he could think of was her sprawled across it in his bed.

The woman came back and he quickly made his selection, then went over. The salesmen had filtered away for a moment and she was by herself, looking in the mirror considering the autumn colored fur enfolding her.

"I like the white better," he said.

"Mmm, maybe." She turned a little, her eyes not leaving the mirror.

"I heard about it."

"And?"

"And you never answered the phone."

"I told you we're done."

"So, you decided to get married."

"Yes. I'll take this one," she said to the salesman who'd come back.

"Very nice, miss. Shall we wrap it?"

She hesitated for a moment, then met Nick's eyes. "I'll wear it."

The salesman smiled. "I'll just wrap up your other coat."

"I have a couple of things to pick up here. Have a drink with me?" he asked when the salesman left.

She was smoothing on a pair of expensive leather gloves. "No. I have to meet Jeb."

"You're really good at giving a guy the brush-off."

She gave a cool smile. "I've had a lot of practice."

"And Jeb? Why him?"

"He can give me what I want."

"Can he?" Their eyes met and he felt the same heat that'd been between them from the start.

She shrugged. "If I'm wrong then it's nobody's problem but my own." She picked up her purse. "See you around."

He watched her walk away, the beige high heels making her long slim legs seem even longer. The salesman brought her bag to her and she got on the elevator. She didn't look at him again, just straight forward. An icy goddess. She really was good at giving him the brush-off.

He went back to the counter and picked up his package, then stopped back at the perfume counter. By the time he stepped out into the cold, evening was falling. A thin band of orange was the only thing separating the purplish sky from the horizon. She passed him in a beige Cadillac, not blinking an eye. Jeb was treating her good. Maybe he was giving her everything she wanted.

Maybe taking up Moriarty's offer wasn't such a good idea after all.

CHAPTER TWO

Delphine Chalmers pulled the letter out and unfolded it, looking over her shoulder as she did it. Her heart was racing. It was stupid and she knew it, she'd be at work in just a little while where she could look at it all she wanted but she needed to read it, just hold it in her hand for a minute.

"*Sweetheart,*
It won't be long now. I love you. Somehow I'll work this out.
G."

Her eyes lingered over the words, the hope that they brought filling her, giving her life and lifting the heavy, choking mantle of reality from her. Her thoughts wandered to the look in his eyes when he'd slipped that note to her, pressing it in her hand when he'd thought no one else was looking, the terrifying fear at being seen mixed with breathless anticipation. It was almost as if she were young again, almost like she'd never...

Her head snapped back and she cried out in pain as her husband's hand pulled her hair tightly. She scrambled reflexively to push the note into her apron pocket before he could see it, but he was too quick for her. He grabbed it out of her hand, ripping it as he did so.

"A note from your boyfriend?" he snarled as his hand fisted. Tears sprung to her eyes. It wouldn't be the first time there'd been a clump of hair torn from her scalp.

"I told you what I'd do if I ever caught you messing around. I warned you. Ya got nobody to blame but yourself, Delphine."

He pushed the note into her lips, mashing her skin against her teeth. She closed them tight, knowing what he was going to make her do. He untangled his hand from her hair, mousy brown threads of it between his fingers, and forced her jaw open, then crammed the note in and covered her mouth with his ham-like hand.

"Eat it. Ya wanna have him so much, eat it," he yelled at her. His always sweaty face was red, the veins in it throbbing and his dark eyes bulging under dark angry brows.

She could barely move her mouth or breathe from the pressure of his hand. It was like a vise. The counter dug into her back. Panic gripped her as she fought to get a breath and her hands tried to pull his away, but he was too strong. The part of her brain that could think made her try to chew. Finally she just swallowed the large hard lump.

"Filthy, fucking whore." He removed his hand from her mouth and instantly cracked it across her face. She sucked in air and staggered against the counter.

She knew it was going to be bad, worse than usual, and tried to curl herself into a ball in the corner, but he grabbed the back of her shirtwaist and held her up. He punched her hard in the chest and gut, working her over like a rag doll until he landed one that hurt so bad it made her throw up.

He let go of her, holding his hands up in disgust. She dropped to the ground on all fours right in the middle of it.

"You filthy, fucking pig! Why I let you stay around, I'll never know." He threw a dish towel at her. "Clean it up, fucking cunt. And get t' work. You're probably gonna be late again. Man, if you lose that job, I swear I'll..."

He banged out the back screen door and she stayed on all fours waiting for the sound of their old DeSoto to go down the street. Each breath felt like the muscles were being pulled from her ribs and she tried to breath slowly, hoping the pain would ease. She didn't cry. She hardly ever cried anymore. It was as if Al Chalmers had drained every tear from her in the first few years of their marriage. All she could feel was grateful that it was over, that he hadn't finally killed her, and that there was still a chance that she would be able to leave him. The thought brought her back to the present. She pulled herself up and nudged on a tap with the back of her hand, rinsing off the puke. She glanced up at the clock and saw that she was already late. The mess was quickly cleaned and she went into the bedroom to change. The baskets of clothes fresh last night from the laundromat still sat in the corner waiting to be ironed. She sighed as she pulled out one of the dresses. It was horribly wrinkled, but it would have to do. She had to get to school before she did get fired. Slipping on her loafers and a coat, she was halfway to the elementary school before she realized that there was still traces of dried vomit on her legs. She almost hoped that she didn't see Grant that day. It would be too humiliating.

"You're late," Nora Hudgens, the school dietician, commented as she took her place at one of the big steel prep tables. "I thought we worked out that little problem. And look at you." The woman tsked disapprovingly as she looked up and down at the wrinkled dress. "I should send you home."

"No, please. I'm sorry. It was the alarm clack. It didn't go off. I'm sorry." She babbled, saying anything and knowing how stupid she sounded. That was the part she hated, sounding stupid, feeble. Her eyes burned but she didn't cry. You didn't let feelings follow you into work. That would get her fired for sure.

"Well, I'm docking you an hour. I can't have people being late all the time. Maybe that will help you to remember. There's plenty of others who'd like this job if you don't, Delphine."

"Yes, Mrs. Hudgens."

The cafeteria boss moved on to her office and Delphine let out a deep breath. She was here. She was safe and she hadn't lost her job. Al would be angry over the docked pay, but it wouldn't be too bad. She concentrated on the mountain of potatoes in front of her and started peeling. Eleven thirty and a hundred hungry kids would come quickly. There were always extra mouths to feed when they made turkey and mashed potatoes. The kids that normally packed their lunches always bought on that day. Somehow, that always made her happy. She'd never had a child. At first, it'd made her sad, but after a few years with Al, it was a blessing. Her thoughts strayed to the kids who came through her line and she smiled a little. Even the bruised ribs and sore muscles didn't take that from her. Working in the school cafeteria was a little like feeding her own kids. Sometimes she'd fantasize that they were hers and that she had a big loving family. It was harmless and filled the hole in her life. It'd given her a reason for living for a long time. That is, until Grant. Now he gave her something to live for.

Eleven thirty came and went. When he came through her line, their eyes met just briefly.

"Everything looks real good today," he said as he smiled at her. The look in his eyes made her know that he wasn't talking about the mashed potatoes and gravy.

She smiled back at him. "Thanks, Mr. Stone."

That was the extent of what they could share together during the space of the day. He moved on as the next person took his place. He sat with the other teachers and staff facing her. Again and again, they would steal glances of each other as he ate, and she put scoops of potatoes on kids' melamine trays. He finished long before the last child had gotten their lunch and she just caught the quick look he sent back to her as he placed his tray in the dishwashing area. His eyes held as much longing as she felt. They had to be so careful. Lunch was over by twelve thirty and then there was a mountain of dishes, wiping down tables, mopping floors and emptying the garbage cans. It was two-thirty before she stepped out on the back dock area and lit a cigarette. It was cold out and she wrapped her arms around her body. She hadn't bothered with a coat. The cold air felt good after the heat of the kitchen.

"Tastes good, doesn't it?" her friend, Joyce, said as she came out to join her.

"Yes."

Joyce lit her own and took a deep drag. "I heard Hudgens today. You gotta be careful, Delphine. You gotta stop coming in late."

"I know." Her eyes looked off in the distance. There was nothing to look at except a chain link fence and a bunch of leafless shrubs with little red poisonous berries that foretold the coming of winter.

"What's going on?" Joyce asked. "I know there's something. You aren't somebody who does this kind of stuff, coming in late, risking your job, looking like..." she dropped it there, the bounds of friendship not allowing her to be so blunt.

"Looking like I just fell out of bed?" She dropped her cigarette butt and crushed it with the toe of her shoe. "Maybe I'm just a lazy piece of shit," the frustration of her situation coming out.

Joyce sucked in her breath. "Wow. Never thought I'd hear you say something like that. What's wrong, Delphine? Come on, tell me. We've been friends since high school. Maybe I can help."

"It's nothing. I'm going back in. Gotta get home and get dinner going. See you tomorrow." She abruptly headed back in. It felt bad, like she was being rude to her best friend, but she couldn't tell her, couldn't open her mouth. She knew what would happen if she did. Joyce would be sympathetic, but the lure of passing on gossip would eventually be too much. Joyce would tell someone sooner or later and everyone would know, then she'd be too ashamed to be seen. She knew. She'd imagined telling Joyce a hundred times and each time the thread led to a place where she ended up with even less than she had now.

Better Joyce thought she was rude than know the truth.

"I know it's Al," Joyce called after her. She paused for the briefest second and then kept going.

The locker area for the cafeteria staff was off the loading dock down a small hall behind the storage area. Everybody but herself and Joyce had already left and the lights had been turned out. It was a little creepy along the shelves stacked high with canned carrots and creamed corn and applesauce. The hum of the giant freezer was the only comforting thing.

"Del," a deep masculine voice whispered.

She peered into the dark and knew who she'd see. It was him. He took her hand and pulled her behind the shelves.

He bent to kiss her, but she put a finger to her lips. "Joyce is still here," she said softly.

Without a word, he led her further back, back to where the bags of potatoes and onions were stacked, the darkest corner and then took her in his arms again. This time he did kiss her and she gave herself up to him.

Odd that they were like teenagers in the first heat of romance. It didn't seem to matter that they were old. Their bodies were no longer the firm fresh flesh of youth. There was age and wrinkles, but it didn't seem to matter. They wanted each other with just as much hunger as when they'd been sixteen year olds after a sock hop.

They were noiseless in their passion and she kept one ear open for Joyce, only really relaxing when she heard her friend's locker open and close and her footsteps fade away from the cafeteria. He'd sensed that too and waited until then to unbutton her shirtwaist. She'd almost forgotten the beating of that morning, but when his hand grazed her ribs she sucked in her breath and flinched.

'What is it?" he asked and then peered down at her body. There was barely any light, but even in the dark, the deep purplish bruising already showed.

'"It's nothing," she said and took his face in her hands and kissed him.

"He hurt you again," he said and she could see the frustrated anger on his face. "I want to kill him."

"No," she whispered back to him, "don't let him take this from us, too."

His fingertips gently traced her ribs and then went to her face. "I love you so much, Delphine. I should've married you."

"I don't have much time," she reminded him. She didn't want to dwell on what they should've done a long time ago. She wanted the piece of him that she could have now.

He bent and kissed her and undid his zipper. Her body was more than ready for him. They made love against the wall of the cooler, sacks of potatoes the only witness to hear the muffled groans behind tightly closed lips. Her body crashed into waves of release quickly, but the ache for more of him didn't quell. He drove deeply and pounded her hard against the cold wall and she wanted more. When they were finished, they leaned against each other sweating, their chests heaving as they caught their breaths. Her ribs didn't hurt.

"I love you, Delphine," he said as his fingers intertwined with hers above her head and he bent to kiss her again.

"Grant." It was all she could say. She wanted him so much. And he seemed to feel the same. It was over too quickly. They both needed more.

"We shouldn't," he breathed, his breath warm against her ear.

"I know," she said and slipped her arms out of her sleeves. A moment later, she stood naked before him and began to undo the buttons of his shirt. He looked down at her, his eyes dark with passion. She swallowed hard, her fingers trembling a little as she worked to undo the last of the buttons. It was a ridiculous chance they were taking. Anyone could walk in on them. He'd lose his job and it'd be a scandal like nothing Owego had ever seen, but it didn't matter. They had to have each other. He laid his jacket on the cold cement floor and she laid down.

"You're so beautiful," he said.

She reached up and took his hand, pulling him down on top of her. They took their time this time. She liked seeing the rise and fall of his shoulders over her body, feeling her legs holding his, feeling the bunching of his muscles as he loved her. That too was over too quickly, but when it was done, they lay together for a few moments pretending that they were lovers who were able to be with each other.

Her fingertips grazed the salt and pepper hair on his chest. "He made me eat your note," she said with a small little laugh.

He took her hand. "I hate that bastard. I can't stand you going through this anymore. I'll find you somewhere else to stay."

She pressed her fingertips over his lips. "No. I have to go home, Grant. You know that. If we both lose our jobs, then what will we do? No. We have to stick to our plan. It's the best way."

He lifted her hand to his lips and kissed it. "Why are you always right?" He paused, then added. "But someday I'm gonna put that guy in the hospital."

"Someday, he's not going to matter anymore."

He left before she did. It was important that they were never seen together. She watched him go before she put her clothes on. He turned to take one last look at her and it made her feel good that he still loved seeing her naked.

She got dressed quickly and a few moments later was reaching into her locker to grab her coat when something fell on the floor. She stooped to pick it up and as she did, the hair on the back of her neck stood up. It was a picture, blurry, dark, but of her and Grant against the cooler. It was them, that day.

She felt sick to her stomach and had to close her eyes for a few moments to ease the nausea. Her mind reeled. This wasn't the first time someone had left something disturbing in her locker. It had started with notes, nasty, insulting notes like a teen-aged girl would write to a rival. Then a series of things that she'd thought she'd lost, an earring, a barrette, a scarf. These had always been wrapped like presents, like some twisted party gift from a sick mind. Then a few months ago there'd been the worst. She remembered it really well. They'd served roast beef at lunch that day. When she'd opened the white butcher's paper, a lot of blood had seeped out of the meat. That afternoon, there'd been a baby doll in her locker, one of those little ones like from Newberry's, and it'd been covered in that blood. She'd recognized the smell of it. Now this.

She looked around, suddenly scared. This wasn't just a demented prank anymore. Someone was watching her, purposely scaring her. Worse yet, someone who knew about her and Grant, but who?

CHAPTER THREE

Jill looked out over the auditorium. The school board meeting was crowded, more than she expected and it was a little daunting. Jeb put his hand gently at the small of her back. "Over here, honey."

He led her to a seat and they settled in. After helping her with her coat, he draped the mink over the back of her chair.

"You sure are a knockout, honey," he said to her.

She smiled at him. "Thanks, Jeb."

This was part of getting her used to what her place was going to be. Jeb Burks Sr. was a school board member and Junior was expected to take his place there when he'd established his own household. That's where she came in. It was her job to charm every old cat in town into accepting her. Not an easy job when you came from the block and Rusty and Hank were sitting in the Marble Lounge every night. She could almost feel the thoughts of the people there. *"What is she doing here?"*

She glanced over at him. Jeb was a sweet guy. After some cold, hard thought, it was the reason that she'd decided to set out after him. She wanted a good guy, a nice guy, a guy that wasn't going to throw her any curve balls. He was about as different from Nick as possible and reminded her a little of George Goble, with his crewcut and shy manner. Funny thing was, he was only really shy when he was around her, almost like he was in awe of her, like she was some sort of crystal vase that he was afraid of breaking. Not like Nick. Nick hadn't been afraid of breaking her. Far from it. Her body reacted at the mere thought of their one night together. It was something she'd revisited a lot over the past few months and it hurt every time. This afternoon had been hard. She'd seen him in the mirror as soon as the elevator doors had opened. That queer shivery feeling had gone through her immediately. It'd been a long time. A long time of dodging her thoughts and then there he was, tall and dark and handsome, like a hard, cold slap coming out of nowhere. Within her reach, but not for her.

Yeah. You think you can just walk away from something like that, something that moved you to your core, but she was beginning to wonder if you could. Sometimes when she looked in the mirror at herself she was afraid that she'd still be longing for the sight of him forty years from now.

"Okay, honey?" Jeb asked.

She nodded and gave him a bright smile. "Of course. This is interesting. I never thought so many people came out for things like this."

He chuckled. "You don't have to lie. We'll get out of here as soon as we can."

Her smile warmed. She really did like Jeb. "I'm fine. Really. And I meant it. I am interested. I remember Mr. Stone from when I was a kid."

"Grant deserves the job."

"I always liked him. He was real nice to me." And that had meant a lot as a poor kid growing up on the block.

Jeb nodded. "I liked him, too. He sure waited a long time for this."

Jeb's father slid into the seat next to her. "Hello, doll. It's not a done deal yet. Ted Kelly is leaning towards that new guy, thinks he's more modern, better ideas. What does Ted know?"

She glanced over at the man Jeb Sr. was talking about. Ted Kelly was a tall, lean man with short sandy hair. He was an IBMer and she'd heard plenty about his flings with secretaries in the beauty shop.

"Some people mistake age for inability."

"Not me, honey. I know some young people with lots of ability." He looked at her pointedly and grinned and she knew he had a few sleazy thoughts of his own. It didn't bother her. She knew how to handle him. It was the sneaks like Ted Kelly that she hated. They were the kind that if you brushed them off, they'd do something to hurt you, really hurt you. Jeb Sr. would just laugh and try again.

The auditorium was filling quickly. Tonight was a "meet the candidates" night.

Both men would be giving their little spiel of why they'd make the best school superintendent. Afterwards would be a coffee and cookie hour where they'd glad-hand the public.

Jeb was talking to the guy next to them and she busied herself with watching the people. From the looks of the women there, it was easy to see why they might not like her. She was Sophia Loren in a crowd full of June Allysons. That was too bad. She wasn't going to change.

She glanced over at the clock and realized that it was ten of seven.

"Excuse me for a minute, Jeb. I'll be right back."

He nodded. "Sure, honey." Then turned back to the guy next to him. They were deep in conversation about the merits of the new Buicks.

She got up and realized that Jeb Sr. had left too. Probably out talking to some of the other board members.

She walked up the aisle looking straight ahead, but knew that she was leaving a bunch of stares in her wake. The creamy wool sweater dress mixed with her curves was hard to ignore. It was the effect she wore it for.

She walked past the cafeteria. They were setting up for the meet and greet. Delphine Chalmers was putting out plates of cookies and they both nodded to each other.

Even with the makeup, she could see the trace of a bruise on Delphine's face. Al Chalmers was quite a guy. They were her parents' ages and Al had been a regular buddy of Hank's. She'd seen them sitting together on barstools laughing at each other's stupid jokes on more than one occasion when she was a kid. She'd always wondered why Delphine had stayed with him. She'd heard her story, of course, just like everybody else had. The story of how Grant Stone had dumped her before he left for Harvard and ended up marrying Mildred Albright, whose father was the head of the school board. He got a job with the school and she got a life sentence with Al.

It must be a pretty hard pill to swallow, working under the guy you once loved and stuck with some jerk, but she didn't feel sorry for her. She didn't feel sorry for any woman who made stupid choices. They deserved what they got. That was why she was staying as far away from Nick DiPaulo as possible. She'd had her fill of stupid choices.

The ladies room was empty. It was the tenth time today for her and she wondered once again when she should tell Jeb. He'd be happy, overjoyed probably, and be more than willing to move up the wedding date. After adjusting her stockings and smoothing her dress, she stepped out of the stall and looked at herself in the mirror. It didn't show yet. If she was lucky, with a good girdle, she'd stay thin until the seventh month. To any of the old bats who asked questions, maybe she'd be able to pass off the quick weight gain to new married life. All that mattered was that Jeb thought it was his and she was going to make sure that he did. She wasn't going to have her kid treated like second best. Her kid was going to grow up in a nice house with proper parents, wearing the right clothes, taking music lessons and going to the right places. That hard shell that she kept around her hardened a little more. She could see it in the mirror as she touched up her lipstick. Her eyes looked hard, just as hard and cold and empty as the inside of her felt, but that was okay. Her kid was going to have a good life, the life she never had. Nothing, and no one, especially not some guy who made her hot just by looking at her, was going to change that.

The halls were deserted and she decided to slip out the exit for a quick smoke before going in to listen to an hour of boring speeches. She was just inhaling her first puff when she heard Jeb Sr.'s voice coming from somewhere nearby.

"Are you fucking crazy, Stone? I've put out money to see that you get this job, big money, and I've stepped on some valuable toes. Nobody uses me like that and gets away with it."

"I never asked you to, Jeb. Besides, this is my business, not anybody else's."

"That's real funny. I seem to remember a discussion we had about a bus contract."

"I only said that I liked your figures, Jeb. I never promised anything. You know that."

The principal sounded like a man up against it, somebody who'd made a deal with the devil. She felt sorry for him. In her book, he was a good guy. Anybody as good to kids as he was didn't deserve to be in a fix.

"I know that when I expect a guy to do something, he does it, and he doesn't screw it up on purpose."

"Think what you want, Jeb. It's my life. You might throw your weight around down at the car lot, but not here. Here, the taxpayers make the decisions. Now if you'll excuse me, I've got a speech to make."

The elder Burks gave an ugly laugh that chilled her. "Yeah, well, we'll see what the board says when I leak a little something into the right ears. Maybe the other guy will be somebody who knows how to treat friends."

She threw the butt on the ground and crushed it, then hurried back in before she was seen. She was in such a hurry, she nearly ran right into Stone's wife.

"Well, look at you," Mildred Stone looked her up and down. "Isn't this a little dull for you, Jill?"

She knew Mildred Stone and had never liked her. She was one of the ones with money, one of the upper class who'd always looked down on her, one of the ones she was going to live amongst.

She pasted a smile on her face. "Not at all."

Mildred gave a strained smile, her faded blue eyes cold. "Don't feel that you need to attend these, dear. I'm sure Jeb isn't marrying you for your civic interests."

Mildred walked away and she realized that her hands were clenched. She flexed her hand and exhaled. It would get easier. They weren't all like Mildred Stone. They couldn't be. Besides, who gave a damn. Jeb looked over at her as she slipped into her seat.

"Everything okay, honey? You look a little pale."

She smiled at him. "Fine. I've got a little surprise for you."

He grinned like a kid. "What is it?"

"After the meeting." She slipped her arm through his. "Something I hope will make you happy."

"Anything you give me will make me happy."

I hope taking on another man's kid will do it, then.

Jeb Sr. took his seat a few moments later and she glanced over at him. He still looked angry.

The crowd began to quiet as the moderator began to make introductions. Jeb

Sr.'s problem was his to deal with. She had enough of her own.

CHAPTER FOUR

"Son of a bitch," Nick muttered and turned the key again. The car gave a faint grind that slowly petered out to nothing. He tried again. There was an even fainter grind. Finally it altogether. He let go of the key and smacked the steering wheel. "Son of a bitch!"

What the hell was he going to do now? He glanced down at his watch. It was already past noon. He'd had a late start getting out of the office and even if he left now it would be a close cut to be on time for dinner.

He got out of the car and went back into the office.

"Forget something?" Johnson said as he flung himself into Moriarty's chair and picked up the phone.

"Car won't start."

He called Hertz, then Avis. Not one car available for the weekend. He even tried the car lots to see if they'd rent him one. Even the garages were booked solid. He went through every dealer he could find in the Triple Cities and was left staring down at the one big ad in the yellow pages he didn't want to see. It was the last place he wanted to go for help.

Finally, he just dialed the number. He was a big boy. He could handle it.

"Burks' Auto. What's your pleasure?" The guy on the other end said.

"Do you have any cars that I can rent for the weekend?"

The guy on the other end chuckled. "Sorry, buddy. Not unless you wanna buy one."

"It might come to that. I don't suppose anybody's around that could take a look at my car. I'm supposed to be in DC tonight."

"What kind of car?"

"An MG."

"Sorry again, buddy. We only service Buicks and Mercurys"

He rubbed the back of his neck. "Look, I'd make it worth your while. Literally, my life depends on it."

The guy chuckled. "Your anniversary?"

"No. Worse. My mother's birthday."

The guy laughed harder. Great. He thought he was some kind of mama's boy. What the hell. He felt like one right about now.

"So can you give it a look or not?" he interrupted the frivolity on the other end.

"Yeah, we'll give it a look. Where are you?"

He gave the address and the guy let out a low whistle.

"That's gonna cost you an arm and leg."

"Yeah, I know. Just try and hurry."

He hung up and waited, the guy's laugh running around in his head. It was over an hour before a tow truck pulled up.

"Have a good weekend," Johnson said absently when he left.

"Yeah."

Buzz, the guy he'd talked to on the phone, took a look, adjusted a few things, tried to start it, then slammed the hood down and wiped his hands on a rag. "We're gonna have to tow it," was his verdict.

Traffic moved around them, some tooting horns, some just giving dirty looks. Thursday afternoon. Women hitting the sales at Fowler's, trying to get home to make dinner. It didn't faze the mechanic. Nick pulled his collar up and smacked his gloved hands together.

"Damn. You're kidding, right?"

"Nope. Needs a new alternator. Gotta do that in the garage."

"Shit."

The guy grinned. "Yeah, stinks, don't it?"

"Yeah. It stinks." This was going to go over real well.

"Hop in, buddy. I'll give ya a ride."

As it turned out, Buzz had a long history with cars of all types, which he was happy to share with him all the way to Owego. They were driving down Main Street when he saw Bennings up the street.

"Hey, can you let me off here? I'll wait in the bar. Just give me a call when it's ready, ok? You know the number?"

"Yeah, no problem, buddy." The tow truck ground to a stop in front of Benning's and he got out, handing the guy a fiver.

"Thanks, pal. I owe you."

Buzz laughed. "Yeah, ya do."

The tow truck rumbled off and he stood outside of Benning's slapping his hands together as he watched his MG disappear down the street. One last look and he went inside. It was exactly as he remembered it. Ralph was there at the bar watching a replay of last night's game and absent mindedly moving a white towel over the bar.

Ralph looked up as he came in and a smile broke across his face. "Howdy, stranger. Haven't seen you in quite a while. What d'ya been up to?"

He slid onto a barstool. "Not a lot. Working."

"Up with the bigshots, huh?" Ralph slid a napkin down in front of him. "Beer?"

"Might as well. Whatever's on tap."

Ralph poured a foam-topped glass and placed it on the napkin.

"Thanks." He picked it up and took a drink. It was going to be a long afternoon. Might as well get the worst of it over with now. "Got a phone?"

Ralph motioned towards the back. "Over there."

He took his beer and went over, closing the door behind him. He dialed the number and waited. Finally, a man's voice came on the line.

"Hi, Stevens, is my mother at home?"

"Yes, sir. I'll get her for you."

A couple of moments later, his mother got on the line. "Don't tell me," she said.

"I know, mom. Sorry. The car died on me. They're looking at it right now, so maybe I'll be able to be down later." He could almost see the smile on her face, the smile she always got when he messed up.

"Your father won't be pleased."

He felt his mouth tense. "I know. I'm sorry I can't be there for you."

He heard a slight sigh. "Always the two of you butting heads. Well, come when you can, darling. I love you."

"Love you, too, mom."

He hung up the phone feeling like a heel.

"You look like a man with troubles," Ralph said when he went back to the bar.

"Crapped out on my mother's birthday." He drained his glass. "Pour me another."

Ralph did.

He ordered some of Bennings' famous fried chicken and they spent the rest of the afternoon watching the game, making the occasional comment, laughing at a joke. The bar was empty and he liked the companionship. Ralph was a studied pro at making a guy feel at home. He caught himself wishing Jill would walk through the door more than once. He even caught himself looking out the big plate glass window for a glimpse of her.

Around four, the phone rang and Ralph handed it to him. "The garage."

It didn't take long to hand it back.

"They have to order the part. Guess I've gotta get a room." He tipped the glass up again.

He went to the phone booth again and looked up the number for the Sunrise.

"Hi. I need a room, probably for the weekend."

"Sorry, sir. We haven't got anything."

"You're kidding. Nothing?"

"Like I said, sorry, sir."

He tried the Deep Well and got the same story. Well, that was that. What the hell was he going to do now? He walked back out to the bar. A few people had strolled in by that point, one of them being Struble.

"Hey, long time no see," the young guy with the brush cut said.

"Hi, Struble. How's life as the chief?" Struble had been promoted after Bently's death. A good choice, even if the kid was too young. At least he wasn't crooked. Not yet.

"Not bad, not bad. Patty and I are getting married in a couple of weeks."

"Congratulations. She seems like a nice kid."

"Yeah, she's pretty excited. Most of the time she's out looking at furniture or wedding stuff. Leaves me a little free time," he chuckled.

"Don't happen to have a spare bed, by any chance? Looks like I'm stuck in town for a few nights. My car died."

The kid's face lit up. "Come stay at my place. Just moved into the new apartment. It's pretty good size and we just bought a new couch. You'll be the first one to try it out."

"Patty won't mind me sleeping on her brand new couch?"

"Nah. Anybody else, she'd throw a fit, but she likes you. Besides, it's my last few weeks as a bachelor, might as well live it up with someone who knows how."

He grinned. He could just imagine that shy, little Patty giving Struble hell about his other friends. "All right, if you're sure it's okay."

"It'll be fun. Maybe you can give me a few pointers."

A few pointers on how to piss off your boss and ruin your career, maybe.

"Let me buy you a beer," he said.

Ralph poured another and set it before the police chief. They'd just settled into talk about the upcoming Giants game, when the bell over the door chimed again indicating another customer. He glanced up to see Jeb Burks walk in. Great. The day was complete.

The bar was filling up with the after work crowd, but Jeb came right over to him. "Nick DiPaulo?" he asked.

"Yep, and you're Jeb Burks." He held out his hand. "Thanks for taking my car in at the last minute."

Jeb shook his hand. "That's what I came to see you about. Geez, I'm awful sorry the guys couldn't fix it up for you right away. They should've called me, you being such a good friend of Jill's and all."

Good friends?

Jeb leaned in a little, lowering his voice. "Jill told me what you did for her and I don't forget something like that. Anybody that treats my girl special is okay by me."

He wanted to pop the guy. "Thanks, Jeb. Just doing my job."

Jeb chuckled and he felt like a jerk. He seemed like a good guy. A nice guy. The kind that Jill should be with. Sure as hell not some guy like him.

Ralph handed Jeb a Manhattan and he took a sip. "Sounds like a line from Dragnet," Jeb laughed. "Listen, how 'bout you come on over tomorrow morning and I'll let you take the pick of the lot, you know, as a loaner, and tonight, let Jill and I take you to dinner, on me, just to show my appreciation."

His appreciation for taking the future Mrs. Burks to bed? He'd take the car, but dinner with Jill? No dice.

"Yeah, thanks, Jeb. I'll take you up on the car. I'm grateful. Thanks. But Jill probably doesn't want some cop tagging along like a third wheel for dinner."

Jeb swallowed some more of his drink, then bit the cherry off its stem. "She'd love it. Give her a chance to show off her new coat. Between you and me, she's a knockout in it."

Yeah. He already knew that. Maybe he oughta go to dinner with them. Maybe seeing Jill in her new life, with a good guy, was what he needed to finally get her out of his head.

"Okay. Thanks, Jeb.

Jeb set his empty glass on the bar and peeled a few bills off the wad he pulled out of his pocket. "His tab's on me, Ralph."

Before he could argue, Ralph looked over at him with a knowing smile. "Sure thing, Jeb."

Ralph knew the score. He'd been around the block a few times, too.

They went out into the cold night and he pulled his collar up. The wind was really whipping and he felt chilled after sitting in the cozy warmth of the bar for so long.

"My car's right over here," Jeb said, pulling the keys out of his heavy overcoat as they crossed the street to the big new Buick.

They drove up Church Street, but didn't stop at Jill's old apartment. He half expected to see her through the big picture window, working late, but the building was dark.

"Jill meeting us?" he asked.

"Oh, no. We're picking her up. She's at the new house, fixing it up and all that. I wanted her to do whatever she wanted to it. Between you and me, the kid's had a hard life. I want to treat her like a princess."

He wanted to pop the guy one. Again.

They crossed the bridge and headed into the new development. There were several houses under construction, a few finished ones, mostly cookie cutter replicas of Better Homes and Gardens knock-offs. Burks pulled up in front of a modern split level with a turquoise door, white siding above fieldstone. There was a pool out back and, from what he could see, there was some landscaping that probably looked good in the summer. An apple tree that maybe someday one of her kids would swing off of.

"C'mon in," Jeb said, "she's probably still getting ready."

They went up the slate walkway and rang the bell. He heard her footsteps and felt like running away. What the hell had he been thinking?

"You don't need to ring, Jeb...," she said as she answered the door.

Her words hung in the air as their eyes met. It took him back to the first time they'd looked in each other's eyes and he knew she felt it, too.

"I brought a friend," Jeb went on, oblivious to what was going on between them. She tore her eyes away from him and smiled at her fiancé.

"I can see that. What a surprise." Her eyes met his again, but by this time the usual cool curtain had come down separating them.

"Hope it isn't too much of a surprise," he offered.

"Of course not," she said as she led the way up a short set of stairs and into the main living room. "Jeb's a very gracious man."

"I told him you'd probably still be getting ready. You go ahead and finish up, honey, and I'll fix us a drink." A kind of goofy grin lit up his face. "We've got some special celebrating to do."

"Yes, we do. I'll only be a few minutes," she said and gave him a quick kiss.

By the look on Jeb's face, he knew she'd done that for his benefit.

"What the celebration for?" he asked.

Jeb handed him a drink. "My baby just told me some good news. Bottoms up," he said happily.

They went to Augie's on Endicott's north side. He wouldn't be surprised to see Cassetti. At that moment, he'd rather be sitting down with the mob boss.

"Great steaks here," Jeb said as he opened the door for her and helped her out.

Jill focused her attention on her fiancé, taking his arm and smiling up at him. They were seated in a booth. The room was dark paneled wood, with a nice bar. A jazz combo played and there was a small dance floor. Under other circumstances it would've been a nice little place.

Dinner was about as uncomfortable as he'd expected it to be, with Jeb, the happy buffoon, eternally oblivious to the electricity between him and Jill. They ordered steaks and shrimp cocktails. The waiter brought their drinks while they waited. Another Manhattan for Jeb, a Martini for Jill and Scotch for him. He downed his quickly. Jill sipped hers and continued to ignore him. The dance floor began to fill up.

"Hey, why don't you take Jill out for a dance. I'm not much of a dancer," Jeb said, a happy grin on his whiskey-flushed face.

He looked at her. Her eyes were cool, inscrutable and he couldn't tell if it was dislike or anger.

"Nah, I'm not much of a dancer either," he said.

Jeb laughed. "Go on. Come on, she'd love it. Wouldn't you, honey?" Jeb turned to her like a puppy looking for approval.

"Of course, Jeb," she said.

He stood and held out his hand as she slid out of the booth. He followed her onto the dance floor. It was impossible not to notice the sensual flow of her hips in the black sheath. She was classy in her black dress, high stilettos and pearl earrings, her hair done up in a twist. She looked like a model, one out of Vogue, but he never wanted to reach up the skirt of any of them and unhook their stockings. He took her in his arms as the slow, sexy bossa nova surrounded them.

 She didn't waste time. "What are you doing here?"

 "Maybe I wanted to see that mink again."

 "You're real funny. I don't want you here."

 "Are you sure?"

 "Yes."

 Their eyes met and he knew she was lying. They both did. He held her closer and felt the warmth of her skin through the sheer jersey.

 A few moments later, her tone was softer, not a lot, but enough for him to hear it. "Look, just don't screw it up for me, okay?"

 His lips brushed her ear and he felt the goosebumps on her arm. "If that's really what you want. baby."

 The music ended before she had a chance to do anything but look up at him with those beautiful green eyes, except this time, they looked a little lost, a little frightened. They went back to the booth just as the waiter was placing steaks on the table. Jeb was right. The steaks looked great. Too bad. To him, it tasted like cardboard.

The ride to Struble's was the longest twenty minutes of his life. He almost had to laugh. Never thought he'd lose a woman to a used car salesman.

He leaned in the window to say goodnight. "Thanks for dinner, Jeb. It was a really great place. Goodnight, Miss Kaufman. Congratulations on your engagement."

Jill gave him a quick glance but said nothing.

"Glad you came with us," Jeb said, then, "Hey, what's going on up there?"

He turned. Up ahead, there were flashing red lights and a crowd of people standing outside on the sidewalk.

"I don't know."

It was Struble's address. He jogged down the sidewalk and pushed his way to the front of the crowd.

"Struble?" he asked, but nobody seemed to hear him. He saw Patty up ahead looking dazed and went to her.

"What happened?"

"He fell...off the roof..."

She looked like she was about to pass out and he put an arm around her waist. "Here, sit down." He helped her onto the front step and sat down next to her, removing his coat to put over her shoulders. "What the hell was he doing on the roof?"

"Fixing the antenna. He wanted...to...watch...the game," she began to blubber and he had to keep himself from chuckling. Struble had probably come home a little drunk and decided he knew exactly what to do. He'd have given ten bucks to have seen it. It'd probably been something right out of the Marx brothers.

"Is he all right?"

She sniffled and wiped her nose on her sleeve. "I think he broke his leg. The doctor's in there with him. He told me to wait outside."

"Good old Struble," he said.

CHAPTER FIVE

He went to the hospital with Patty and made sure she got back to her parents' house afterwards. His car problem was handled when she handed him the keys to Struble's.

"Here, take them," she said. "I know Gary would want you to use it while he's laid up."

"You sure, Patty?"

She managed a tired smile. It was after four in the morning. "I'm sure. Besides, this way you can visit him. He'll like that."

At least it'd be easier visiting Struble than it was Moriarty.

The phone rang at six-thirty. Struble's couch was a lot more comfortable than he'd expected or maybe it was the six Scotches. Either way, he'd just fallen into a nice deep sleep and didn't want to hear a phone ringing in his ear. Shit. It might be the hospital.

"Hello," he mumbled, his eyes still closed.

"Chief Struble?" the voice on the other end asked.

"No. Friend of his."

"Oh, well, do you know where he is? We've got an emergency here."

His eyes began to open. "This is Agent DiPaulo, FBI. Chief Struble had an accident last night. He's in the hospital."

He sat up and reached for a pack of smokes, lighting one as the voice on the other end continued.

"Oh, boy, we got a problem, Agent DiPaulo. I gotta talk to the chief."

"I don't think Struble's gonna be up to it today. Broke his leg. Anything I can do?"

"Somebody died, a teacher, but..."

"But, what?"

"Something's wrong with it. Can you take a look at it before I let them take the body. I'd feel a lot better if somebody with a little experience saw this."

He was already beginning to pull on his pants. "Sure, I'll come take a look. Wherabouts?"

"The Pink Prison...sorry, the elementary school, over on Main, by the theater. You can't miss it."

He knew the building. Like a cake of Pepto Bismol sitting on a little rise above the town. "Pink Prison". Funny. Kids had a great way with nicknames.

He drove up the long driveway and parked behind the police car. Officer Ford was standing at the door to the school looking about as nervous as a twenty three year old kid could look who'd just seen a dead body.

"The kids won't be here for a while. This is Principal Stone. I called him right away."

He shook hands with the tall grey-haired man. He looked like a principal. Serious.

"I didn't know if I should close the school or not, officer."

"Let me take a look, first. Don't let anybody in yet." He told him.

The principal nodded. Underneath the chiseled jaw he looked jarred, too.

Kids' gaudy finger paintings lined the walls amongst civil defense signs and fire drill instructions. The school was quiet, its light brown speckled tiles shiny and clean. It was a bastion of order. And now there was a dead body. Probably some teacher'd had a heart attack or something and he'd be through in five minutes. Ford led him downstairs into the bowels of the school, where the shiny tiles left off and dull grey concrete took their place.

"In here," Ford told him as he ducked under big pipe.

They entered the boiler room and he saw legs sticking out behind the massive furnace. A man with a bald head stood nearby, just shoving a stethoscope into a black bag.

"She's dead all right," the coroner told him. "I didn't touch anything though. Didn't like the looks of it."

He nodded and went around the corner. Ford and the coroner were right. Something was wrong with this picture.

His first response would've been to laugh. It was a grotesque picture, almost comical, if it weren't so creepy. The woman's dress was pulled up, exposing utilitarian undergarments that his grandmother might have worn thirty years ago and thin legs encased in heavy stockings, but that wasn't what had troubled the people who'd seen her. It was her face. Someone had taken lipstick and drawn a clown's exaggerated big red lips on her and a small black moustache. It was like something a kid would've done, like a picture one of them might have drawn on the blackboard to mock her.

He bent down on one knee for a closer look. She was older, a thin wrinkled bag of bones. There was no wedding band and her clothes were what anyone would expect of an old maid schoolteacher. A dark blue polka dotted rayon and low black heels that tied. Serviceable, not made for fashion.

He took a good look at the face underneath the paint. There was no hint of any other makeup, no lipstick on her lips, no rouge, no mascara. Her brows were unplucked and even in death she looked like she had a perpetual frown. Her features reminded him of the Wicked Witch of the West. In spite of, or maybe because of, the caricature, she was a figure of tragedy. It struck him that here was a life that had never really been lived.

Something caught his eye and he looked closer.

"Hand me a plastic glove, will ya?" he asked the coroner.

He slipped it on and gently moved her lip. They were stained with a reddish substance on the inside.

He rose and pulled off the glove. "I think you're gonna need an autopsy done," he told Ford. "And have somebody come over to take pictures."

Ford looked anxious. "Um, that would be me."

"Okay. Go grab your camera. Make sure you get all of it, her face, the clothes."

"Yes sir." Ford hurried off.

They left the body with the coroner and he went out to speak with the principal.

It was light out, past seven, and he really wanted a cup of coffee. A few teachers stood huddled together shivering, curious looks on their faces.

"What time do the kids get here?" he asked the principal.

"Eight, some a little before. I can't have them seeing this, Agent DiPaulo."

"Is there a back entrance?"

"Out by the gym. It opens onto the street behind us."

"Can you keep the kids off the ground floor until I give you the all clear?"

"I think so. I'll post Mrs. Flood, my secretary and Mr. Boyle, our gym teacher at the top of the stairs. I'll take Miss Gibney's class myself today." Principal Stone glanced over toward the teachers. "What should I tell them?"

"Just tell them there's been an accident and not to mention it to the kids."

The principal nodded and they went their separate ways. He got back in the car and watched the women hurry into the school, followed by the principal. If he wasn't mistaken, the principal seemed a little nervous, the kind that people show when they have something to hide. He started the car. The day was young. Professional courtesy first. Time for a hospital visit.

His nickel rattled down the slot, a cup dropped and black steamy liquid filled it. He took a sip. Maybe he was getting too used to machine coffee. It actually tasted good. He ambled down the hall to Struble's room.

"So, how's the patient?" he asked.

Struble's brush cut stood up in odd spikes and looked like even more of a kid than he was. A nurse finished taking his blood pressure and left. Not before giving him a flirtatious smile. Nurses. Every guy's fantasy. Too bad he was loopy from the pain killers.

"It hurts like hell," Struble said with a goofy grin.

"At least it's only up to your knee. Nice job on the antenna, by the way."

Struble chuckled. "I guess I was a little drunk."

He laughed. "I guess you must've been." He took another sip of coffee. "Did Ford call you?"

"Yeah. Thanks for stepping in. Damn, wouldn't you know something like that would happen the night I do this?"

"Always the way. What's the doc say?"

"Gotta keep it up for a week, but then I can walk around with a cane. Gonna be walking down the aisle with it."

He chuckled. "Patty must be relieved, though."

"Well, she's a little upset. It wasn't exactly how she pictured things."

"I can well imagine." Patty had probably pictured him as her knight in shining armor standing at the end of the aisle. Like most women. Like Jill was thinking of Jeb? He doubted that. Jeb was more like a cash register standing at the altar. The thought ticked him off and he changed the subject.

"So, do you know anything about this teacher?"

Struble grimaced and pushed himself up further in the bed. "She's been there a hundred years. Mean old bag."

That fit. She looked like a mean old bag.

"Probably had a hundred enemies then."

"Probably every kid that had her. I know I hated her."

"Good thing you broke your leg then. That rules you out."

Struble frowned, the fog clearing a little. "You really think she was murdered?"

He shrugged. "That's up to you."

Struble was quiet for a few moments. "You know, Nick, when they offered me the chief's job, I was real flattered. Thought I was big stuff, bragged about it to everybody. I'm finding out it's more than I bargained for. Bently was a jerk, but he at least knew what he was doing. I don't know anything."

"Don't worry about it, kid. You'll be fine. Everybody's gotta start someplace."

"Were you nervous the first time you had to investigate a murder?"

He chuckled. "You shoulda seen me the first time I saw a body. You get used to it."

"I don't know," he said skeptically. "I saw that mobster's body. Remember? The one at the Beautiful Lady? I almost threw up."

"The bloody ones are hard to take."

"You don't think you could stick around and give us a hand for a few days? I mean, I can't do much of anything and Ford's even more clueless than I am."

He liked Struble. Always had. What the hell, he'd already missed his mother's birthday.

Might as well screw up the rest of the weekend. He'd send her the presents. She'd understand. She always did. And with any luck, he wouldn't even have to talk to his father.

"Sure."

Ford was beginning to nod off by the time he left. His stomach started knotting before he even pushed the down button on the elevator.

"Come on," he muttered.

He watched the numbers as they crawled upwards to the sixth floor. He didn't want to go upstairs, didn't want to see Moriarty, at least not the way he was right now. He was a shitty friend. The doors opened, he stepped in, took a deep breath and pushed the up button.

He wasn't much changed. Still grey. Still lying there in those cold white sheets with his eyes closed like he was already dead. This time, he didn't try to sneak away. He took a seat next to the bed and waited.

"Couldn't stay away," Moriarty's scratchy voice piped up, his eyes still closed.

"Yeah, that's it. How ya feeling?"

His eyes opened. "How the hell do ya think I'm feelin?"

"Yeah. Stupid question."

"What d'ya want, kid?"

He filled him in on the murder. When he was done, Moriarty cut to the chase.

"Couldn't stay away from that broad, could ya? Well, you're supposed to be the boss, what're ya gonna do?"

He sounded weaker than he had just two days ago but he could still hear the authority.

"It's a murder in a school. FBI can investigate."

"Ya tellin' me you wanna be the boss, now?"

"Yeah, I guess so. You win."

"I knew you'd give in. You're too easy."

"Yeah. That's what they all say. So, what's it gonna be?"

Moriarty gave a weak chuckle. "You're the boss, you tell me?"

"Guess, I'll do a little investigating. So, do ya need anything? Can I get you anything? How about some spaghetti from the Oak Inn?"

"Sounds good, but nah. Think I'll wait. Thanks, though."

He got up to go. "Anything you need, you call, okay?"

Moriarty nodded and he began to leave.

"Go get that broad out of your head," Moriarty called after him.

She's already gone, boss.

When he got back into town, he headed down Court Street and turned onto North Avenue then swung his car into one of the spots across the street from the diner. Best place to get the lowdown on anybody anyway.

The smell of sizzling burgers hit him as he opened the door. It was a welcome smell. Something he felt comfortable with. The easy ambiance of a greasy spoon. He grinned. Wouldn't his old man like that. Bells jangled announcing his entrance and the first person he saw was Helen. Her face lit up when she saw him. The pixie had grown out a little, giving her a little more sophisticated look. He liked it.

"Howdy, stranger." She sauntered over to the booth where he'd planted himself. The noon rush was just starting but she headed right straight for him. It paid to be liked.

"Hi, yourself. How's life?"

She laughed. "Can't complain. Like the new do?"

"I do. Very Audrey Hepburnish."

She laughed again. "Thanks. What'll you have?"

"Coffee."

She gave a little doubtful look. "You look like you could use a little something more than that. How about some pie? We've got apple and cherry."

"Maybe later."

"Suit yourself," she said amiably and left.

He unfolded the newspaper he'd grabbed. Nothing in there yet about the murder. He pulled out his notebook and started jotting down notes.

He was on his second cup of joe by the time the lunch crowd had thinned out. Helen stopped by with the coffee pot. "Top it off or does your stomach hurt enough?"

He put his hand over the top of his cup and grinned at her. "You talk to all the customers like that?"

"No. Just you. So why are you here this time?"

"I got stuck."

She laughed and sat down across from him. "You got stuck."

"Yeah. It's a long story. My car died."

"Here?"

"No. I was in Binghamton. Couldn't find a rental. Only guy that would take a look at it was somebody at Jeb's."

"Well, that's rich."

He looked at her, puzzled.

"You. Jill. Jeb. Don't tell me you don't know."

His jaw tightened. "Yeah. I know. What do you know about a Miss Gibney," he asked, switching the topic, "one of the teachers over at the elementary school."

Her nose crinkled. "That old witch? Couldn't stand her. Why? Did they find kids buried in her cellar or something?"

"Not yet. That's what Ford said. Not on anybody's hit parade, I guess."

"No reason she should've been. Want to know why?

"Sure."

"I'll tell you a story. Jimmy Smith was a kid in my class. His parents were kind of poor, I guess. Anyhow, he didn't have much, his clothes were kind of old, a few patches here and there. I guess it made him kind of shy, embarrassed, you know."

He nodded.

"Anyway. Jimmy had a problem with stuttering. Only when he got real flustered, most of the time he was okay. We were learning times tables. I remember it was after lunch, because I kept watching the clock waiting for art class. I wasn't really paying attention, the words were just coming out of my mouth. When we got done, she told Jimmy to say the three times by himself. Threes were the hardest. We all had trouble with them. Jimmy stood up and got real red and tried to say them, but he started stuttering. She started yelling at him, really screaming, and then came down the aisle for him. I remember being scared out of my wits. She grabbed him by his collar and dragged him up front. She told him to hold out his hand and he started crying. He wouldn't hold it out and the more she yelled, the harder he cried. I remember holding my hands together so tight it hurt, but I was too scared to let go. Anyway, she grabbed his hand and started hitting him hard with her ruler. We heard it smacking his skin. I started to cry, a lot of us did, but we didn't make a sound. The only sound was that ruler smacking his skin and Jimmy crying. It still makes me sick to think about it to this day."

Her face was pale and there was nothing giggly about her expression now.

"Didn't anybody do anything? I mean another teacher or something? Somebody must've heard all this going on?"

"They never did anything. I think the rest of the staff was just as scared of her as we were."

"Jimmy's hand was black and blue for weeks after that." Her eyes met his. "I never heard him talk in class ever again."

"Did you tell your parents?"

"What was the point? Dad would've just said that Jimmy'd probably done something to deserve it and gone on reading his paper and Mom would've told me to stop being dramatic."

"Whatever happened to Jimmy?"

"He quit school as soon as he could. Works over at EJ's."

"What about other kids? Did she do the same thing to other kids?"

"Oh, sure. She made me sit in the garbage can once. Boys got it the worst though. She really hated them."

"Thanks."

Helen got up. "Sure. Any time."

He watched her start to walk away. "Listen," he said, "how about catching a movie this weekend, I mean if you don't have anything else going on." It was stupid and he knew it, but the idea of sitting around the whole weekend with nothing to do but think about Jill didn't precisely appeal to him.

"You're serious?"

He chuckled. "Yeah, I'm serious."

She plopped down across from him once again. "Why?"

He couldn't have been more surprised if she'd slapped him.

"I'd like some company." The words just came out.

She seemed to understand. "Okay. Just friends, then?"

"I'd like that. Just friends."

"Okay. I could use a little company, too." She wrote her address on one of the guest checks and slid it towards him. "Pick me up a little before seven. I like the early show."

With that, she went off, disappearing behind the kitchen's swinging doors, and he felt like kind of a heel, using her to keep his mind off the woman he really wanted.

That feeling wore off by the time he got over to the doctor's office. Ford had given him the address, a big white house overlooking the river. He was a new guy, just moved back to town and autopsies helped pay the bills until his practice got going.

"Really odd, this death," Dr. Carroway told him once they were in the examining room. "Those traces of red around her lips...iodine."

"Iodine?"

"That and a whole lot of booze. Looks like she ingested the iodine with the alcohol. That would've masked the taste somewhat. From the looks of her liver, she drank a lot. Definitely cirrhosis. She wouldn't have had long anyway."

"Do you think it was suicide?"

The doctor gave a small laugh. "There are a lot easier ways. It's possible, but I doubt it. Iodine poisoning is a pretty bad way to go, besides, it doesn't generally cause death. You have to drink a lot of it to be fatal. Although, in her case, with the liver in as bad a shape as it was, it might've worked. Still, she probably didn't know her liver was so bad. Alcoholics generally won't believe it even if they do know it."

"So the cause of death was poisoning."

"Indirectly. There would've been a period of vomiting and delirium. I'm guessing that in her diminished capacity, she fell down the stairs. Look here," he said and pointed to a bloody dent in the woman's skull. "Technically, the cause of death was the blow to her head, but the iodine in her system caused diminished capacity and would've killed her in the next few hours. I'm putting down cause of death as the head injury, but between us, it was the iodine that did it. It'll be listed as suspicious and there'll be an inquest."

He looked down at the woman. The makeup was still on her face, even more grotesque against the death pallor.

"I was about to clean it off," the doctor said. "I didn't want to send her over to the funeral home like that."

"You're probably the only one that would've cared. Did you know her?"

Carroway smiled. "Yeah. She was a mean old bat, but that was a long time ago."

"So you went to school here? Somebody said you'd just moved back."

Carroway dampened some cotton with alcohol and began to wipe off the makeup. "My wife and I left when I went off to med school. We haven't been back since." He gave a little chuckle. "We didn't dare."

His eyebrow rose. "Why's that?"

"I was sixteen when I graduated from high school. My dad arranged it so that I could. Janie and I were dating. About what you'd expect happened. We knew I was going off to Boston soon, got carried away and next thing you know, she's pregnant. Here I am, supposedly some brilliant whiz kid and I'm stupid enough to get my girlfriend pregnant."

He paused to take a look at the woman's face. It was now clean and he covered it over with the sheet.

"Janie didn't tell me right away and she was too scared to tell her parents. I went off to school. Probably we would've forgotten about each other, we were just kids, but I went home at Christmas, couldn't wait to see her. The first time we were alone, I figured it out. I felt that hard little lump in her belly and knew. She started crying, thinking I was going to dump her, but honestly, I was happy. That baby meant we weren't going to drift apart. Janie and I ran off. It was a big scandal. Janie was only fifteen. In the end, her parents gave consent for us to get married. They had to. Her father was the principal."

He chuckled. "That *would* be quite a little scandal."

"It was. Janie's dad was worried about us coming back, about nobody coming to my practice, but we wanted to come home, so here we are."

"And here you are with this."

"It pays the bills." He grinned. "Well, some of them."

"You'll do okay, doc," he said before leaving.

The sky had clouded over into dark grey. Snow was coming. Crossing guards, sixth graders with their white canvas sashes crossing their chests, officious and serious looking, had already stationed themselves at nearby corners. The doctor's office was just a street over from the school and he decided to walk over. The cold air felt good. By the time he started up the long walkway, the kids were coming through the doors, laughing, yelling, walking in pairs and threes. Several teachers stood outside the doors, their coats fluttering in the chill wind, making sure their charges went off in the right directions. The crowd thinned and dwindled to nothing and the teachers went inside, but not before shooting a few curious looks in his direction.

He was going there to see Stone. His secretary was on the phone and he glanced around the office. There were pictures of the school, the kids, the staff. He took one down to take a closer look. Grant Stone, all white teeth and button-down good looks, stared back at him. There were several young women in it, but he and the woman next to him were holding what looked to be some sort of award. It was the expression on the young woman's face that grabbed him. The shyness and intense longing in that face. oh, that's where trouble began. A mousy little creature infatuated with her boss. If he had a nickel for every time that kind of situation caused a shitload of problems that he had to clean up. He highly doubted Stone was having an affair with Sybil Gibney, though.

"Mr. Stone's in a meeting, Agent DiPaulo," the secretary told him. "He should be done in a few minutes if you want to wait."

"I'll wait. Mind if I walk around?"

"No. Go right ahead."

Once again, the school was quiet. Numbers on each of the classroom doors told which grade was in there. Gibney was third grade. He tried the door. It was still locked, just as he'd ordered. Stone taken the kids to the library for their class that day, telling them that they were painting the classroom. He looked around. Light spilled from a doorway further down the hall and he went towards it.

"Miss Latham" the door said in black-edged gold letters. 5th grade.

"Hi," he said from the doorway.

A youngish teacher, her brown hair in a short neat flip turned around from the chalkboard she'd been writing on. She frowned at him over the tops of her glasses. "Yes? Can I help you?"

He pulled out his credentials. "I'm Agent DiPaulo. Mind if I ask you a few questions?"

She turned and began to finish what she'd been writing. "So it wasn't an accident." She gave a little snort. "Seems a little big for the FBI to be investigating."

"Maybe. Do you know anybody who might want to harm Miss Gibney?"

She snorted again and turned around, putting the chalk down in the tray. "Anybody who knew her. She was a miserable drunken old bitch."

He hadn't expected that from the prim schoolteacher in a brown plaid dress. "Sounds like you didn't like her very much. Where were you last night?"

"Thursday nights I have dinner with my mother. I went home about eight and graded papers until around ten, then I did my hair and went to bed."

"Do you live alone?"

"Would I tell anyone if I didn't?"

He waited.

She rolled her eyes finally and gave him a straight answer. "Yes, I live alone. No boyfriend. Okay? Satisfied?"

"Just trying to see where everyone was who thought she was a 'miserable drunken old bitch'."

Her lip curled up a little. "I know. I guess I'm just a little touchy on the subject. My boyfriend and I just broke up. Ordinarily there might've been someone at home with me on a Thursday night, if you catch my drift."

"I think I do. Sorry about the boyfriend."

She shrugged her shoulders and began walking around the room distributing composition books. "It's okay. The competition was too tough. I wasn't in the same league."

"How's that?"

She looked over at him. "Jill Kaufman."

If she'd wanted to shock him, she'd done a good job. She was right about one thing. She wasn't in the same league.

"So you were dating Jeb Burks?"

She nodded and brushed past him on her way back to the desk. "I thought it was going someplace, and it might've, but suddenly Jill was on the market. But then, you know all about that, don't you."

Her eyes met his.

"I know that things changed for her."

The girl gave a phony laugh. "Yeah. They changed. Anything else?"

"Is there any reason in particular that you didn't like Miss Gibney? Had she done anything to you?"

She looked thoughtful and her face softened a bit. "Not especially. I mean, she didn't beat me out for a promotion or anything like that. The thing is, in a way, there were times when I kind of felt sorry for her. I think I understood, a little, of why she turned out that way." She began to put on her coat. "All I've got to say is that I'm not going to let that happen to me."

"What do you mean?"

"I mean, I think a man did that to her." Her mouth hardened again. "Well, I'm not going to let one do that to me. Now, if there's nothing else, I'd like to get out of here."

"Nothing for now. Thanks."

She tied a bright orange scarf around her hair, then picked up her purse and a bunch of papers.

"Can I help?" he offered.

"I can manage."

She said it with kind of a grim determination and he knew she meant it about more than just carrying papers. Her heels tapped down the hallway and he heard them go down the stairs and then the big oak door open and close. He wondered if Miss Latham would end up like Sybil Gibney. Somehow, he didn't think so and he kind of felt sorry for the man she did end up with. There'd be a lot of thawing needed. Maybe she was a lot more in Jill's league than she thought.

Stone was done with his meeting when he returned to the office.

"Thanks for waiting for me," he said.

"No problem, Agent DiPaulo." The principal waved his hand towards a chair. "Have a seat. You can leave, Miss Flood. Have a nice weekend."

"Thank you, Mr. Stone. Goodnight, Agent DiPaulo. Dreadful thing about Miss Gibney...," she twittered out the door. Stone closed it behind her.

"She knew Miss Gibney from years ago," he said as he took his seat behind the large desk. "They started at about the same time."

"Ah. I see. And you? Were you here then, too?"

"No. I started a few years later. I think Sybil had been here, oh, for maybe two, three, years."

"And what did you think of her?"

Stone became guarded. "She was a good teacher," he hedged.

"You mean she wasn't a 'miserable drunken bitch'?"

"Where did you hear that?"

"Was she?"

If possible, his expression became even more hidden. "If she was, I was unaware of it. As I said, she was a good teacher. She'd been here for many years and was well-respected. Now, if there's nothing else…"

"Yes, there is. Where were you last night?"

"Here. The Board of Education meeting. It was a `meet the candidates' night. I'm one of the candidates for superintendent. You can ask any one of about a hundred people who were here."

"And afterwards?"

"The meeting lasted until about nine-thirty. I left and went home." He smiled. "I'd say that my wife could vouch for me but she was already in bed. A cold."

He nodded. "Okay. So was Miss Gibney at this meeting?"

"I assume so. it was expected that all the teachers would attend, though I didn't actually see her myself."

"I'd like to take a look in the classroom."

"Of course." Stone reached in his pocket and pulled out a keychain. "I'll let you in."

It was a short walk down the hall. The principal opened the door and flipped on the lights. Rows of kid-sized desks faced the front of the room where the teacher's desk stood. On each desk was a small, square white cardboard box with a big red cross. From a kids point of view the room must've been imposing. He glanced at the walls and noticed it right away. The pictures, or lack thereof. The kids' artwork was missing. The walls were a blank dull green. Books lined the shelves, but he saw the difference from the other classrooms. They were all in a line, but it reminded him of houses he'd seen where the kids were left to themselves. The titles were upside down, some stuck out more than others. Kids that were doing their best to comply. He knew something about that, about trying and failing.

"Nobody's been in here?" he questioned.

"No, I made sure it was locked myself. Miss Gibney and myself, and of course, the janitor, are the only ones with keys."

"What are the boxes for?"

"Our school makes first aid kits for the Red Cross each year. It helps the children understand about helping others. It's part of our civics lessons. When they're finished with them, we send them off to wherever the Red Cross wants them. This year it's China."

"Ah." He picked one up and opened it. Gauze. White tape. Aspirin. Iodine. Twenty-four kits, twenty-four bottles of iodine. Enough to make someone very sick. Maybe even very dead. That kid, Jimmy Smith, flashed before his mind.

"You can go if you want," he told the principal. "I won't be long."

Stone nodded. "Take as long as you need. Just lock the door on the way out."

"I will."

"Good night, then."

"Good night." He waited until he heard the principal's footsteps go down the hall before opening the drawers.

It didn't take long to find her stash. He pulled out a bottle from her desk drawer and stared at it. It was empty, but that wasn't what bothered him. He couldn't put his finger on it for a minute and then he knew. He picked up one of the kits and sat down at her desk.

Presumably she left the meeting and came up to her classroom to drink. What then? Did she just decide in the middle of the thing that drinking iodine was the thing to do. He pulled the small brown bottle out the box and held it up to the light. It was empty all right.

He sat back in the chair and looked out over the desks. Okay, so maybe she was tight and stupid and decided to drain twenty-four bottles of iodine, what then? Did she get up and neatly put them all away, then put her empty vodka bottle in the desk drawer, take a stroll down the hall and fall downstairs into the boiler room? No.

He glanced over at the haphazard rows of books again. He pictured it. Sybil, drunk, probably pissed off about something as only an old, mean drunk can get, tearing through the boxes looking for the iodine, throwing stuff on the floor. If Sybil Gibney had done this on her own, there'd be stuff lying all over the place. And her empty vodka bottle wouldn't be neatly back in her drawer.

Someone else had been there.

CHAPTER SIX

Chuck Ford was at the station bright and early the next morning. "Got the list of everyone that was at the school that night," he said as soon as he walked through the door.

"Thanks. Any coffee?"

Ford grinned in that wobbly Adam's apple way of his. "Sure thing. Comin' right up." Chuck dropped the file on his desk and took off. He hung up his overcoat and sat down. Now that it was Struble's, the chief's office looked a lot different from when it'd been Ed Bently's. No Playboys, everything neat, tidy. A picture of Patty on the desk. He picked up the file Ford had left for him and started looking though it, making a few notes in the margins.

Ford came in with the coffee.

"Thanks. Close the door. Looks like it's gonna take a while to get through all of this. Good work, by the way."

"Thanks," Ford said with a pleased smile and left him to it.

He took a sip of the coffee. "Damn, Ford, I might just see if I can get you a job with the agency."

Contented with the decent cup of joe, he went to work.

The problem was that there were a lot of people in that school that night. Almost anybody in town could've spiked her bottle. By all accounts, she was enough of a lush that she might not have even noticed. Stone, all the teachers, the board of education, Miss Flood, even Jeb and Jill. It seemed that the only person who wasn't there was Helen. And that kid, Jimmy Smith. Maybe it was time somebody talked to him. Get some inside lowdown.

Since it was Saturday, he expected to find Jimmy at home, but his mother told him that he was working an extra shift until noon. EJ's was down towards the new high school. Kids had to pass it on their way. Probably more than one parent threatened their kid that if they didn't get decent grades they'd be working in the shoe factory. He parked outside the long brick building and waited. The whistle blew and workers started filtering out. He checked the picture Jimmy's mother had given him and picked him out right away. He looked young, even younger than Helen. He was kind of hunched over against the wind, hands in his pockets. He got out of the car and walked towards him.

"Jimmy?"

The kid looked up. "Yeah?"

"Can I talk to you for a couple of minutes?"

"Y..y..yeah."

"I'm Agent DiPaolo. FBI." He showed him his credentials. "Let's go grab a cup of coffee."

Jimmy nodded, looking scared.

"Don't worry. You're not in any trouble. I just need some information."

Jimmy nodded again, but still looked wary. Life wasn't easy for this kid.

He drove them the few blocks to the diner.

"How about some lunch?" he asked after they'd eased themselves into a booth. "My treat."

"Uh, thanks," Jimmy said quietly. He was exactly like Helen had described him. She wasn't working that afternoon. It was somebody he didn't know. They made small talk until the waitress brought their burgers and Cokes.

"Miss Gibney died the other night," he started. "I'm handling the investigation while Chief Struble's laid up."

Jimmy chewed and swallowed. "I heard about it."

"The grapevine moves fast around here."

"Yeah, I guess so."

"I heard she was pretty rough on you."

Jimmy played with one of the fries. His eyes didn't leave the plate. "I guess."

"It's okay, Jimmy. I'm not going to ask you about what she did. You don't have to tell me anything you don't want to. I'm just interested in your opinion."

"My o..o..opi..nion?"

"Yeah." He pushed his plate of untouched fries towards Jimmy. "Have these too, if you want."

"You sure? Okay, thanks." Jimmy dumped some ketchup on them and kept eating. He was one of those skinny guys who could eat a horse.

"You weren't at the school the night she died, but you probably know most of the people who were." He passed the list across the table. "If you were to pick anyone on this list to have killed her, who would you pick?"

A sort of smile cracked on Jimmy's face. "You're kidding. I don't know anything about this."

"I know. Just pick one. Look at the list. Go on. What the hell, live it up."

Jimmy's grin widened. "This is crazy." He looked down at the list, frowning a little and moving his lips as he silently read the names.

"Gee, I don't know," he said, pushing the list back across the table. "How about the principal. It's always somebody like that."

"You didn't like Principal Stone?"

"He wasn't the principal then. He was our sixth grade teacher. But, yeah, I liked Mr. Stone." He frowned. "I don't think Miss Gibney did though."

"Why do you think that?"

"I saw her go to his room once. I was down in the foyer waiting for one of the other kids. Mr. Stone's room was at the top of the stairs. The door was closed but I could heard that they were arguing. I remember hoping that my friend would come because they were scaring me."

"Could you tell what they were arguing about?"

He shook his head. "Sorry. Maybe I was just too scared."

"Well, thanks. You've been a big help."

Jimmy chuckled. He seemed like a nice guy. "I didn't do anything."

"Yeah. You did."

He dropped Jimmy off at his house and then headed over to Front Street. He stopped in front of the principal's house. It wasn't much of a start, but it was something.

The door was opened by a well-kept, middle-aged woman in a grey silk day dress. Her steel grey hair was perfectly waved and her face was made up sedately, in keeping with her age. Her expression said it all. He didn't belong there and wasn't welcome. "Can I help you?" she asked with a prune-like purse to her red lips.

He had her pegged the second she answered the door. He'd grown up around women like this his whole life. Old money women who thought that everyone, including their families, and especially their husbands were beneath them. He already knew Grant Stone's life must be a living hell. The surprising thing was that it wasn't this woman laid out on the Doc Carroway's autopsy table.

"I'm Agent DiPaulo. FBI." He showed his badge. "I was wondering if I might have a word with Mr. Stone."

"Of course," she said as he entered the large foyer. She led him down the hall to a oak-paneled library. "I'm sure the two of you would like some privacy. I'll go get him."

She left and he looked around the room. It reminded him of his father's, not that he'd spent much time there.

Stone entered shortly. "Ah, Agent DiPaulo, what can I do for you?"

"You might want to close the door, sir."

Stone's brow rose a little, but he did as he was asked then took a seat opposite him. "So, what's on your mind?"

"I want to know more about your relationship with Miss Gibney."

Stone spread his hands. "I'm not sure what I can tell you. We worked together."

"Sybil never married."

"No."

"Why not?"

Stone smiled. "I try to stay out of my colleague's lives. I'm sure I don't know. Perhaps she wasn't interested in marriage. She was very dedicated to her job."

"Yeah. About that. You said she was a good teacher. She beat kids. Humiliated them.

Explain to me what part of being a good teacher that is?"

Grant wasn't smiling anymore. His square jaw had tightened. "What do want me to say?"

"How about you start with why you were covering up for her, why you didn't fire her."

"You're a smart man, Agent DiPaulo. You know how things work. You know I couldn't. She had tenure. Besides, it would be a huge scandal."

"So, you were afraid of a scandal?"

"Scandals damage a lot of people, most of them unintentionally. Think about it, the school fires a teacher for abusing students. Then parents don't trust any of the teachers, their kids see this and then they stop obeying. Once discipline is out the window, there's chaos in every classroom. Yes, all right, I knew what she was like, but I knew things would be worse if I tried to fire her."

He sat silently for a moment, allowing the principal to stew in his juices.

"You know, I know men like you. You're not a bad guy. You probably really care about these kids. It was probably killing you to keep her on. But what you just said is a pile of bullshit. You know it and I know it." He leaned forward. "Now, I'm going to find out one way or another what was really going on. It'll be easier if you tell me yourself. Especially since, as you said, you want to avoid a scandal."

Stone buried his head in his hands. "I knew it would come to this," he said softly

He waited. The guy would spill his guts when the time came. When the principal looked up again, he looked haggard.

"I didn't mean for it to happen," he said.

It didn't take a rocket scientist to figure out just what "it" was.

"So, tell me about it."

"It was years ago, ancient history. It just happened once."

"Look, your ancient history doesn't seem very ancient right now, so go ahead, tell me what happened."

Stone rubbed the back of his neck. "I got drunk, real drunk, one night. Mildred and I...we were having some problems. Anyway, I stopped off at the school. I was going to sleep it off there. Parts of it are a little fuzzy. I was pretty drunk that night. I kind of passed out and then all of a sudden Sybil was there. She wasn't like how she is..was..now. She was nice, not really pretty, just kind of a shy pretty. You know what I mean."

He nodded. Yeah, he knew what he meant. There were thousands of them out there. The ones you never really give a second glance to, and then, if for some reason you have to, you see that there is a little something there. Not much, but something.

Grant continued. "I knew it was wrong, knew it before it even happened, but I knew how she felt about me and it'd been so long since..." He paused.

"Yeah, I get it. A long time since you got laid and there was some girl ready to give it to you."

"Crude, but to the point."

"Then what? How long did it go on for?"

"Just the once. Like I said, I knew it was wrong right from the start."

"And so she just let it drop? That was the end of it?"

Stone started squirming again. "Not exactly."

"How, not exactly?"

Stone let out a breath. "A few weeks later she told me she was pregnant."

"That must've sent you for a loop. What'd you do?"

"What could I do? It wasn't like I could marry her. I offered to help her, you know, to do whatever she needed to do, but she said the only thing she wanted was my promise not to fire her."

"So let's see if I've got this straight. You bang this lonely teacher, get her pregnant, she turns into a drunk and you let her terrorize a bunch of kids so that you can do the `honorable' thing?"

"It sounds pretty bad put like that."

"Don't worry about it, Stone. There's a few million other guys walking around in your shoes. The thing that concerns me is that maybe you got a little tired of covering for her, maybe you didn't like the idea of your granddaughters sitting in her class one day. Yeah, that's right, I know about your daughter and son-in-law."

Stone's face tightened. "Janie and Alan shouldn't have come back here. Small towns have long memories. But as for the girls, I can ease your mind on that score, detective, they're enrolled in St. Pat's. I would've never allowed them to be exposed to..."

"A miserable old drunk?"

Stone nodded. "I know it was an awful thing that I did. I wish I hadn't. I should've protected those kids all those years, but I swear I didn't kill her. I suppose, God forgive me, I hoped that she'd just drink herself to death one day and now she has and I don't feel anything but relief."

"Well, that's honest at least. What happened to your kid?"

"She gave the baby away. That's when the drinking started." He continued on, "I used to think that I was the one who ruined Sybil's life, and I take responsibility for part of it, but I realized that her life had been ruined long before me."

"Why do you say that?"

Stone got up and began to pace, rubbing the back of his neck. "I'd be in my office and sometimes I'd see her go back to that dark, cold house at the end of the day. She looked so small, so frightened. Once, she hesitated before going in. She looked back towards the school and you could see how much she didn't want to go in." He paused. "I heard bits and pieces of what life was like for her, how she was never let out to play with others as a child. The only time she was ever allowed to leave home was went she went off for her teacher's training. You know, I saw pictures of her then. She looked...happy. Then she came home, and all this happened."

He left Stone stewing in his own guilt. Stepping onto the wide porch, he pulled his collar up. The wind had picked up since he'd gone inside. It was colder and grey. Seemed like once November hit Owego, there was nothing but grey. He burrowed into his coat and looked up at the sky as he walked to his car. Looked like snow was coming. In DC they were probably just wearing sweaters. Even that thought didn't make him wish he'd made it down there that weekend. His jaw tightened. He still had his father's phone call to look forward to. The old man wasn't going to let an opportunity slide to give him hell.

It took just under an hour to get a signed search warrant in his hand. Lucky for him that the judge was a Giants fan and didn't want to miss the game that afternoon.

He stood outside Sybil Gibney's house and looked it over. She lived on Main Street, near the school. The house looked like something out of Poe and he was pretty sure that bats lived in that attic. The house itself was painted grey. A few bare shrubs completed the picture. Since none of her things had been moved out of the classroom, he'd been able to snatch the keys out of her purse.

He let himself in and shut the door quietly. Funny how even when you knew nobody was around, you were always quiet when walking around a dead person's house.

The first thing that hit him was that it looked it'd been frozen in time, like nothing had changed since the turn of the century. He walked through every room getting a sense of who she was and how she lived. Stone had been right. It didn't take long to figure out that she'd led a very closed, solitary life. The only thing missing were cats. Usually women like this had about fifty cats. There were none. Nothing that said life existed in this house and he was getting the creeps. He opened the refrigerator. Not much in it. A little milk. There was a stained cup on the counter and a coffee pot. The only dish in the sink was a glass. He lifted it and took a sniff. Booze. A quick glance at the garbage can told him there were at least five bottles in there. She was a vodka girl, through and through.

He went upstairs. Most of the bedrooms were dusty, untouched. In one of the rooms, he picked up a picture that looked like it must've been her parents. Two unsmiling people dressed in clothes from the twenties, the man in a suit with a starched white shirt, the woman in a plain, boxy dress, her hair pulled back away from her face, exposing features that were just as drab as the picture. A little girl stood somewhat behind her mother's chair with big round staring eyes. He opened the drawers. There were still clothes there, old, maybe from the thirties. Ma Gibney hadn't gone in for anything fancy in the way of underwear, that was for sure. As he left he noticed a cross-stitch hanging on the wall by the light switch. It said "Obey".

"This place would make one hell of a haunted house," he murmured, still quiet.

The other bedrooms were barren of anything besides heavy old furniture. Everything was faded. Drapes, carpets, bedspreads. Again, the life drained out of them. No wonder Sybil Gibney drank.

Sybil's room was only differentiated by the fact that there was an alarm clock and two bottles of vodka on the nightstand. It had the same narrow Victorian bed and faded coverings as the other rooms. He picked up one of the bottles. It was half full, the other still had the seal on. Unlike most long-time drunks, she hadn't graduated to the really cheap stuff yet.

The dresser and wardrobe held a few depressing variations of the same clothes she'd been found in. Cheap rayon dresses and undergarments devoid of any touch of femininity. By the end of this, he was going to need a drink. He lifted the lid of the small pink leather jewelry box on top of the dresser. Inside was a picture of a shyly smiling young woman holding a newborn, a curly lock of baby-fine blond hair tied with ribbon and a folded paper. He pulled the paper out and unfolded it.

It was a birth certificate. "Baby boy. Born August twelfth nineteen thirty two." Mother was listed as Sybil Smith. Father was listed as unknown. A sad start for any kid. He looked down at her face. What it must've done to her to give her kid away. He thought of Jill and how young and frightened and hurt she must've been. It made his stomach tighten. He wanted to protect her, but that was another guy's job now. He put the certificate in his pocket and took the box.

There was only one bedroom left. From the doorway, it looked the same as all the others. He went to the nightstand and pulled the drawer open. The first thing he saw made him let out a low whistle.

"Well, Sybil," he said slowly.

The cover of the magazine showed a woman tied up in a leather bra and panties, her backside prominently displayed. Could be just stuff she'd taken from kids over the years, he reasoned after getting over the initial shock. The next thing his hand touched told him that it was more than that. He pulled out an impressively large piece of male anatomy done in beige rubber.

    He held it up. "Hmm. Impressive."

    He put it back in the drawer and looked through the rest of the room. Apparently, Sybil enjoyed two things in life, booze and porno, though why she kept them in separate rooms left some lingering questions. Maybe because she didn't like what she'd turned into. Maybe to pretend she was someone else, with someone else. Who knew. One thing was for certain, he thought as he rifled through the magazines and books, her collection would've made a sailor blush. It also explained the absence of cats. No need for cats when you've got all that rolling around inside your head. He shoved the things back in their respective places. Finding out her hobbies didn't really do much to tell who might've murdered her.

    The attic door was across the hall and he climbed the rickety steps, brushing off cobwebs as he did so. By the amount of dust, she hadn't been up there in years. Nothing much of interest, old furniture, some old trunks with the usual assortment of family debris. A pile of Liberty magazines sat next to a stack of National Geographics. He picked one up. It was from 1910. Nothing much of interest. He went downstairs to the first floor again. The door to the cellar was off the kitchen. There was no rail going down the stairs. They were old and creaky but no cobwebs. She'd been down there. Often enough that there wasn't much dust.

He pulled a string attached to a single bulb and his skin crawled. It was like the scene in "Psycho" when the detective finds the mother. He kept expecting Sybil's mother to be sitting down there in a rocking chair. The light didn't reach too far into the dark corners and he heard skittering. Mice. He looked around for a flashlight. There was one laying on an old truck. It worked. There was an old monster of a furnace, the kind you found in a tenement or some old apartment building. It was cold. Either she'd been too broke to turn the heat on or was so drunk most of the time, she hadn't noticed the cold. He'd bank on the drunk part. Old furniture, trunks, barrels of old crap. Lots of empty bottles. He focused the light towards an old strongbox. Now there was something interesting. A brand new Yale padlock.

He reached into his pocket. Sorting through the keys, he quickly found one with "Yale" stamped on it and tried the lock.

"Wow," he whispered.

It wasn't just a few old records. There was a lot more. Pictures. A lot of pictures. He sifted through them, looking closely at one in particular. It looked like it could be Grant Stone and he wasn't grading papers in it. There were others in a similar vein, but different people. Looked like his girl was a blackmailer. There were other things, too. Letters. Documents. She must've had a grip on half the town.

His hands combed through the rest looking for something to show where the child had gone, but no luck. Still, it was evidence and he'd gone through it again over at the station. He picked it up and was about to walk upstairs when suddenly a sharp, cracking blow crashed into his skull, the world went strangely out of focus and he fell forward into blackness.

Pain brought him back. His head felt like it'd been split in two and he didn't know how long he'd been out for. Not more than a minute or two. He got up on all fours and had to shut his eyes to keep the waves of dizziness from making him fall over again. He took some deep breaths and, holding his head, slowly got up. He looked around trying to remember where he was and then it came to him. The lockbox was gone.

He climbed the stairs. Whoever had knocked him out hadn't worried about him following. The door at the top wasn't locked. When he got outside to the porch, he looked up and down the street. There was nobody, not even a car. He felt inside his coat pocket and smiled. At least they didn't have the birth certificate.

CHAPTER SEVEN

"Gee, what happened to you?" Ford asked as he walked past him to Struble's office.

"Nothing." He rubbed his head and for the first time noticed there was blood on his fingers. "You got any alcohol around this place?"

Ford grimaced. "Looks pretty nasty, Agent DiPaulo. Sure you don't want the doc to take a look at it? I got him right in the other room filling out some papers."

He looked up. "Why? What happened?"

"Aw, nothing much. Got in a little fender bender off Main Street. Guess he was in a hurry and ran the light. Oughta be more careful though. He'll be making his own patients." Ford chuckled.

"Off Main Street, huh. Yeah, ask the doc to come take a look. Hey, and Chuck, just call me Nick. No sense standing on formalities."

Ford grinned. "Sure, Nick." The sergeant went off to get the doctor and he touched the back of his head once again. Whoever'd smashed his head in had done a good job of it. It hurt like a son-of-a-bitch. And why the hell was Alan Carroway speeding down Main Street at just about the moment his assailant must've been getting away?

Ford came back. "Sorry, Nick, the doc's gone. Want me to call his house? He's probably on his way home."

"No. I'll be okay. Just get me the alcohol."

He sat back in his chair and closed his eyes. Ford came back with the alcohol and some cotton and started cleaning off his wound. He winced.

"Does Doc Carroway get many tickets?"

"None as far as I know. He must've had something on his mind." Ford finished up and threw the used cotton balls in the garbage. "Anything else?"

"Just some coffee if there's any made."

Ford got him his coffee and shut the door, leaving him to himself. The mysteries just kept piling up like pieces of dogshit in a kennel. Sybil had been blackmailing people, and it looked like a lot of people. That right there was enough to get anybody iced. He was going to have to find that lockbox and he had a pretty good idea of who might have it. The thing was, what big secret did Carroway want to protect? Everybody who gave a damn already knew he'd knocked up the principal's daughter. That was old news. He pondered that as he sipped his coffee and stared at Patty's photo. His mind wandered and he wondered what it'd be like to have Jill's photo on his desk in some office. Dream on, buddy. That wasn't happening in this lifetime. Maybe on Jeb Burk's desk, not yours. He glanced over at the clock. It was nearly six. Better get his ass in gear and get cleaned up. He didn't need Helen getting curious about dried blood all over his head.

"The Magnificent Seven" was playing that night. It was a busy night at the Tioga. A Saturday night in November, the options were limited in Owego. At least it was a western and not some Doris Day fluff. Not that Doris wasn't a hot little number in those frilly baby dolls she wore, but with the mood he was in, he'd rather see some blood and guts.

"I was thinking you'd probably stand me up," Helen said as they waited in line.

"So, you think I'm kind of a jerk. Thanks." He pulled out a few bills and handed them to the guy at the window. He got the tickets and took her elbow to lead her into the main lobby.

She chuckled. "Yeah, maybe. Mostly, I just figured you'd be pining away for somebody else."

"Do I look like the `pining away' type?"

She eyed him. "Not really, but guys are funny that way."

"How about you? You `pining after' some guy?"

"Yeah. But not the way that you think. I've got my guy, it's just that he's in the service."

"Want some popcorn or something?"

"Sure.," she looked around, "but, it's getting pretty crowded. Let's find some seats first."

"Okay." They went into the dimly lit theater and looked around. "So, where's he stationed?"

They squeezed past a several couples and she settled herself in a seat. "He's shipping out for someplace called Viet Nam. I've never even heard of it before."

He kept his mouth shut. He'd heard of it and from what he'd heard, it didn't sound good. The lights lowered and the previews were beginning. "I'll go get us some popcorn."

He excused himself and went to the lobby. The crowd was thinning and he decided to have a smoke before going back in. He lit up and inhaled, looking out the big glass doors onto the street when he sensed someone nearby. He glanced over to see Jill standing a few feet away. Doc Carrothers and his wife were walking past her and she grimaced.

"Hi," he said.

"Hi." She inhaled from her own cigarette.

"Something wrong?"

"I don't like him. He's a creep."

He looked towards Carrothers who was now sharing a laugh with his wife as they disappeared into the theater. They looked like the All-American couple to him. "Carrothers? Why?"

"It doesn't matter."

"Don't tell me you're here by yourself."

She nodded towards the refreshment stand. "He's getting popcorn. What about you?"

"Helen. Just friends."

"I wasn't asking. She's nice. Does her boyfriend know?"

"Like I said, we're just friends. There's nothing to know."

"Not like us." She slowly exhaled smoke. His eyes were drawn to her neck, that beautiful smooth skin, and her mouth, so soft. He missed it. He wanted it.

"Look," he crushed out his cigarette and met her eyes, "I didn't say this the other night, but I hope you'll be very happy. Really. I mean it."

Jeb came up to them then. "Hey, Nick, glad to see you. Had a great time the other night. Can't wait to see this movie. I hear it's great. Say, we're giving a little party next Friday. Kind of a pre-wedding bash. Jill thinks I'm crazy, but I love to celebrate. We're getting married the week after next, day after Thanksgiving. Why don't you come over for the party? Hell, come to the wedding if you're still in town. We'd love to have you, wouldn't we honey?"

Their eyes were locked with each other and he saw how hard this was for her. He knew then and there just how big a price she was paying to have all the things Jeb could offer her and it hurt him. He wanted to save her from herself, but he knew he couldn't. She'd never let him.

"He'll probably be gone by then,' she said.

He knew what she was telling him. She didn't want him there and they both knew why. He didn't know what made him say it. He guessed he just wanted to see her again before all was said and done. Maybe he was just a jerk. "I'll be there, Jeb." His eyes didn't leave hers.

Jeb clapped him on the back. "Great! Oh, look at me." He laughed. "Left the popcorn right on the counter. Be right back, honey. Nice to see ya, Nick."

He hurried off towards the counter.

"Don't come. I mean it. We're done. We've been done. We were never started."

She ground out her butt and walked away, tightening the belt on her leather jacket.

He went and got the popcorn for himself and Patty feeling like somebody just kicked him in the gut.

The music was starting as he took his seat.

"I didn't know what you like to drink. I got you a Coke."

"Great. Thanks," she said, preoccupied with the intense opening music and Cinemascope. A small village. Good versus evil.

Maybe he'd get some ideas from Yul Brynner, though he was pretty sure he wasn't going to turn Owego into a shooting gallery.

Sybil Gibney had been an evil woman. She'd spent her life hurting the innocent. Maybe she'd had a bad childhood. He didn't give a shit about all that psychological crap. In the end, evil and good were black and white. She'd made her choices and her day was gone. Retribution had come to her. Now he had to clean up the rest of the mess, wipe it clean. Maybe it was because he liked this hick town. Maybe it was because he just wanted to find out who'd done away with the old bitch. Maybe it was because he remembered what it was like to be a kid at the mercy of a teacher like that. Maybe he just liked doing his job.

By the time Charles Bronson was lying dead in the dirt, he'd managed to push Jill out of his head. She'd been right. They'd never started. He had a job to do and then he'd need to ride out of town and into his father's bank.

The lights went up and everyone started to leave.

"I liked it," Patty said as he helped her on with her coat. "What'd you think?"

He thought he needed to find out why Doc Carroway was a creep and he had a pretty good idea of where he'd find out.

"I liked it."

People flowed out onto the sidewalk in front of the theater, some talking about the movie, some deciding where to go for a bite to eat.

"Want to get a drink or something?" he asked.

"No, thanks. Besides, it's not a date, remember?" she teased.

He liked that pixie cut. It suited her. Helen was a cute kid.

"I don't think we'll be breaking any rules if I buy you a burger."

"That's a slippery slope, pal. One night a burger, the next night, who knows?" She laughed. "Besides, you're still nursing your wounds, and that's a dangerous place. I'm not having Jerry get a letter the minute he gets off a plane telling him that they saw me with some other guy in a dark corner in a bar. That's not the kind of girl I am."

He nodded. He respected her. It wasn't every chick that thought like that and he hoped this Jerry deserved her.

He drove her home.

"So Miss Rulebook, do we shake hands or something? I'm a little new at this just-friends thing."

She chuckled. "You're an idiot, but I had a good time. Thanks for the movie."

She hopped out of the car and hurried up her walk. He waited until she was inside, then left. Oddly, it did feel like a date. A date with a girl who wasn't very interested in him.

*****

"This is getting to be a habit," Judge Barton complained the next morning.

The judge had just been sitting down to his bacon and eggs and by the looks of him, he took his food seriously. He led Nick into the library where he'd signed the warrant from the day before and parked himself at his desk to read it.

"Are you going after every decent citizen in town now?" he grumbled as he scratched his signature across the page.

"I'd like to try not to, your honor."

The judge folded the document and handed it to him. "I'll be having a roast beef dinner at two o'clock and I'm sitting down to watch the game at three. I don't expect any interruptions. Do I make myself clear, Agent DiPaolo?"

"Yes, your honor." He slipped the search warrant into his coat and left.

Carroway answered the door with his tie half tied. He finished tying it as he greeted him. "Agent DiPaolo. Hi. I was just getting ready for church. Come on in."

He stepped into the foyer of the large, colonial style house. It was warm and looked like a real family house. He even smelled waffles and coffee. Nice. A family about to go off to church and he was going to blast it all to hell.

"I have a warrant to search the house and your car, Dr. Carroway."

Doc's fingers stopped and his eyebrows rose. "What?"

"This is a search warrant." He handed the paper to him.

Carroway perused it and gave it back. "I don't understand."

At that moment, a slender, pretty young woman appeared in the entrance to the living room. "Alan?"

"Honey. Uh," he floundered.

He took the reins. "I'm Agent DiPaulo, Mrs. Carroway. This is a warrant to search your property and car."

Her eyes flew to her husband. "What's this about, Alan?"

"It's okay. Go get the girls ready. I'll take care of this."

"I'm sorry, Mrs. Carroway, you'll need to bring your children down here. You'll all have to wait here until the search is done."

"Alan?" she asked once again, her face paling.

"Just do as he says, Janie. It'll be all right."

With one last look, Janie hurried up the stairs.

"I don't know why you're doing this. What is it that you think I'm hiding?" The affable doctor was beginning to show signs of irritation.

"You can save us a lot of time by telling me why you ran that red light yesterday."

"What? You're joking, right? I was in a hurry. I was distracted. Geesh, is this what you do to everybody with a ticket? Hunt them down like they're criminals? You're going to have a lot of work on your hands."

"Is that your car in the driveway?"

"Yes. Janie's is in the shop."

"I'd like the keys, please."

The doc fumbled in his pocket. "Here."

He went out to the car just as Carroway's wife and daughters came downstairs. The kids looked scared and he knew that they were watching him. It took all of five seconds. He opened the trunk and there it was. He slipped on gloves and pulled out the lockbox. Once it was locked securely in his car, he returned.

"Got anything you want to tell me now, Dr. Carroway?" he asked.

"I don't have any idea what this is about."

He looked over at the doc's wife. "You're free to go, Mrs. Carroway."

"No," she held her children close. "I'm staying. I want to know what this is about, too."

He sighed. "Yesterday, in the course of an investigation, I was assaulted. The lockbox that I was about to take in as evidence was stolen. Immediately afterwards, your husband was stopped for speeding through a red light in the vicinity of the assault. He said he was `distracted'. I'd like to know your husband's account of that time and why he was so `distracted'."

Janie's eyes narrowed and the expression of her face hardened. He'd seen that transformation before. Wives that already knew the truth. Jill thought Carroway was a creep. He wondered what kind of creep his wife knew he was.

"Yes, what was going on, Alan?" she demanded.

"Nothing was going on. I was in a hurry to get home. I was late. I was thinking about my rounds, Janie. That's all," he said impatiently and turned towards him. "I don't know how that lockbox got in my trunk. Somebody must've put it there. You're the FBI. Maybe you did. Unless you have anything else, we're late for church."

"If that's how you want to play it. You better hope I don't find anything in there that points to you, Doc. By the way, did I mention I found it in Sybil Gibney's basement? If you were messing around there, it'll sure look like you were the one that murdered her. Have a nice day."

He left the house and started down the driveway. He was nearly to the car when he heard footsteps running after him.

"There's something you need to know." He looked back at the house. "I wasn't at Sybil Gibney's. If I have to, I can prove it."

"Okay. Shoot. Where were you?"

"I was with someone. A woman. Janie doesn't know."

The hell she doesn't.

"Who were you with?"

He hung his head and rubbed the back of his neck. "Shit. Can we keep this between us?"

"I'm going to have to talk to her. You know that, Carroway. Come on, just spill it. Better that than a murder rap."

"When you put it that way...her name is Debbie. Debbie Olkowski. She and I, we, knew each other in high school."

"An old flame? Or was this ongoing?"

He shook his head and looked upwards. "Shit. This is a fucking nightmare. You don't understand. Debbie was, is, a friend. It isn't just sex. I had to marry Janie. Don't get me wrong, I love her, but..."

"But you didn't want to give up the other girl."

"Yeah. I guess that's what it amounts to. Please, don't involve Debbie in this. It would ruin her marriage. Hal would never understand."

"Yeah. I can see where that would be hard." He took out a notebook. "What's her address?"

He got all panicky. Not a pretty sight to see a man look like that. "Look, you can't go to her house. At least promise me that."

"Look, Carroway, for all I know, you're the one that tried to split my head open and I'm not in the business of making promises. What's her address?"

"Twenty nine Paige Street."

He shut his notebook. "Okay. Thanks. I'll check it out. In the meantime, stay available."

"Wait. Look. What if I get Debbie to come down to talk to you? Would that be good enough?"

He turned. "Have her at the station tomorrow by nine."

"Okay. I will. She'll be there. Thanks, DiPaulo."

Carroway hurried back up the driveway and he left. He could just about imagine the scene in that household right about now. Perfect little Janie would probably love nailing her cheating husband with a murder charge. Why did husbands always think their wives didn't know?

He drove past The Beautiful Lady on his way back to the station. It wasn't on purpose, just happened to be on the way. Yeah. That's the way he told it to himself. He expected it to be dark with a for sale sign on it. It surprised him that there were lights on and he caught a glimpse of Jill through the plate glass window.

He pulled into the parking lot the wrong way and parked.

Before he could argue himself out of it, he got out of the car and went to the door.

She was vacuuming, her slim body encased in black stretch pants and an overlarge sweatshirt. From the look on her face, her thoughts were a million miles away, somewhere where she had no cares other than just cleaning a rug. Her hair was in a ponytail and she reminded him of a kid in high school. He knocked. She didn't hear him for a minute, kept right on vacuuming, determined to get every last bit of that dirt. Finally, she looked up, frowning a little, as if to say, "who could possibly be banging on my door?". Her expression changed when she saw who it was. Calm was replaced by cool.

"Yes, officer?" she said after opening the door a crack.

"Hi."

"Is that all?"

"Can I come in?"

"I'm cleaning."

He cracked a grin. "I can see that. Can I come in?"

She opened the door and he stepped aside.

He walked around and took a seat in one of the chairs. "Looks nice. Better than the last time I saw it."

"I replaced the linoleum. I didn't want to keep it after..."

"Makes sense. I thought you were done with all of this."

She began to wind the cord up. "I'll never give up my business. So, is there something I can do for you?"

"Why do you think Doc Carroway is a creep?"

She rolled her eyes and dumped a bucket of mop water in the sink. "He's slimy. I don't know. He just gives me the creeps."

"Has he ever done anything?"

"All I know is that I'm never taking my clothes off in front of him."

"Now that's interesting."

She leaned against the sink. "Why? Because you think I'd take my clothes off for anyone?"

"No. Because he's a doctor and I don't make you as being afraid of a doctor."

She snorted. "I'm not afraid of him. I just don't like him. He reminds me of some guy that Goobie Henson."

"Goobie Henson. Now, that's a name. What's his story?"

"He was some jerk that used to expose himself to little kids. He did it to me when I was a kid. I heard he did other stuff, too. There's something about Alan Carroway that gives me the same feeling I used to get when I saw Goobie Henson. Creep radar, I guess."

The chair revolved slightly and he pushed against the floor, moving it slowly back and forth. "Whatever happened to Goobie Henson?"

She began to rinse out the bucket. "He was found on the railroad tracks one morning. Guess he must've passed out on them."

"Or maybe some little kid's father took care of business."

"Cops are always thinking. Yeah. Maybe. So is that all?"

She wanted him out of there. But it wasn't really Doc Carroway or Goobie Henson that he'd come there to talk about.

"Why are you marrying him?"

He heard the intake of her breath. "That's my business. If you're done asking questions, you can go now."

His eyes met hers. "Why didn't you answer the phone?"

"I told you we were finished."

"You also told me we hadn't really started. I wanted to. You did too."

She finished cleaning the sink and put the lid down over it. "That was a mistake. You should forget about it."

"Did you?"

The green eyes softened a little. "No." And, then, "But, I'm going to."

He got up and took her hands in his, looking down at them. "Jill, don't marry him if you don't love him."

She was looking down at their hands, too. He heard a sniff and he saw a tear roll down her cheek. "Please get out," she said in a raspy whisper.

"Jill..." he reached for her and she backed away knocking over a tray in the process. They both reached for the things that fell at the same time and she got the razor first.

He heard the quick hissing intake of her breath as she bit her lip and held her hand. It was dripping blood.

"C'mere." He wound a clean towel around her hand and held it up. "Bandages?"

"Upstairs."

He nodded and followed her up the back stairs to her apartment. It was the same as he remembered it.

"In there," she said nodding towards the bathroom.

She sat on the edge of the tub while he rifled through the medicine cabinet.

"I'm fine. I can do this," she said.

He ignored her and knelt down in front of her, gently unwrapping her hand. She bit her lip again. It was quite a gash, but the bleeding had slowed.

"You might need stitches," he said, looking at it closely.

"No. It'll be all right." She reached for the bandages that he'd set on the sink and he took them from her.

"Hold your hand over the tub."

She did as she was told and he poured peroxide over the cut.

"Ouch!" she pulled back, but he kept hold of her arm and poured a bit more on it.

"'Let it dry," he said and lifted her hand. He blew on it gently, then began to bandage it. As he finished putting the last piece of tape on, he felt her fingers against his hair.

He looked up into her eyes and then bent and touched his mouth to hers. It was warm and soft and he wanted her. Her arms went around him and she met his kiss.

He pulled her up next to him and held her. "I've thought about you a lot, Jill."

He heard her sniff and when he looked at her, her eyes were blurry with tears.

"Don't do this," she whispered.

His hand cupped her face and she lowered her eyes. He kissed her again, wanting to feel her soften, surrender. She did and he realized just how much he'd wanted her over those past few months. He kept kissing her, not wanting to stop. It felt like the most right thing he'd ever done in his life.

He heard her almost imperceptable "no" through the pounding of his own blood.

"I can't," she said.

"Jill..."

She edged back a bit, but his hands still rested on her hips. "I need you." He didn't really know until that moment just how much he meant those words.

"I can't," she pleaded with him. "You've gotta leave."

"Jill, don't do this to us. Don't do this to yourself."

"Please, Nick, just go."

She wouldn't look at him. He dropped his hands and left, not even seeing where he was going until he found himself in the front seat of his car and his hands were clasping the cold hard steering wheel.

"Shit." He smacked the wheel and got out. Ralph Benning got twenty bucks off him that day.

He'd downed another couple of aspirin and was settling in for his second cup of coffee when Debbie Olkowski walked into his office the next morning. Even hungover, he could appreciate the package she delivered. Blonde, that sunny kind of blonde that only cheerleaders seemed to have, she was the kind of woman that every guy had to look twice at.

"Alan said you wanted to see me." She sat down in front of him, the thin fabric of her tight sweater stretching over perfect breasts.

He ignored them and pushed a pad of paper and a Bic towards her. "Write down the date and time of the last three times you saw him."

She frowned a little, but picked up the pen and started writing. When she was done, she pushed it back towards him.

It confirmed Carroway's story.

"If you don't mind me asking, what's this all about?"

"Just confirming your boyfriend's story."

"I see," she said slowly. "Obviously, he's in some sort of trouble. If you don't mind telling me, what is it?" She took out a cigarette and held it between her long slender, perfectly manicured fingers.

He lit it for her. "Sorry, ma'am. I can't do that."

She chuckled and leaned back a little in the chair, her coat falling open a bit more. "Of course, you have to say that. Well, that's all right. I'm sure whatever you think he'd done will get cleared up soon."

She crushed out the cigarette in his ashtray and stood up, tightening the belt of her coat.

"If you need anything else, please call the house between nine and four when my husband's out. I'm sure you understand."

He did.

She left and he kind of felt sorry for her husband. The poor slob probably kissed the ground she walked on. Men were stupid. His jaw tightened. Yeah, and he was one of them. His heard throbbed and he took another sip of coffee. It still didn't tell him why the lockbox was in Carroway's trunk. That was going to take a little figuring.

He'd been too drunk to go through the box the night before but now he hauled it into the station and set it on top of the desk.

"Whatcha got there?" Ford asked with interest.

He pulled out Gibney's keys and opened it. "A lot of secrets, Chuck. Better close the door. There's a lot of people that could get hurt with this stuff."

"Holy crap, Nick!" Ford said when he saw the things in the lockbox. He picked up one of the pictures.

"Yeah. Looks like Miss Gibney knew a lot about everybody." He pulled out the contents and began to sort them into piles, letters, documents, pictures and objects. "Start making a list of these things. I'm going to try to group these by people."

They worked for the better part of an hour. He read through a letter. "Hey, Chuck, who's `Bean'?"

"That's what we used to call the librarian over at the high school."

"Hmm. Bean has quite an imagination." He handed the letter to his sergeant.

"Oh my gosh." Ford's eyebrows rose and he gave a little chuckle.

"Yeah. It's always the quiet ones, huh. You know, there's one thing that bothers me about some of these," he said as he held up a negative to the light.

"What's that?"

"Look." He spread a few of the pictures out across the desk. "Notice anything odd?"

Chuck frowned as he studied them. "Apart from they're all of people with their pants down?"

"Yeah. You know Owego better than I do, Chuck, but doesn't it seem like some of these are a little far afield for a spinster schoolteacher that never went anywhere but school and home? I mean, this guy, I can bet he hasn't set foot in a school in thirty years."

Knowledge dawned. "You're right about that. You can't tell where a lot of these are, but the people, geez, they sure as hell weren't doing this stuff at the school."

"Exactly. There's another thing. I never found a camera in any of her stuff, so unless she hid it someplace, somebody else has been taking these."

"Holy crap, Nick. But then why would this be in her basement? And the key? Didn't you say it was one of hers? Hey, maybe she had an accomplice?"

"I kind of doubt it, Chuck, but maybe. You never know."

The bell at the front desk rang and Ford went out to see who it was. He came back a few seconds later. "I got Mrs. Reynolds and her kid out here. She wants to talk to you and she looks kind of upset."

Ford showed them in and shut the door. Frances Reynolds was a heavy set woman wearing a red tweed coat with a fake fur collar. She entered his office like a bulldozer. Her kid, also fat, looked scared out of his wits. The bulldozer came right to the point.

"Tell him, Toby," she ordered.

The kid looked down, his chubby cheeks pale as he shuffled his feet. "I, uh, did, uh something, uh, to Miss Gibney."

He raised an eyebrow and sat back. Well this was a twist he hadn't been expecting. "What did you do, Toby?"

"Tell him," the bulldozer ordered.

The kid took a deep breath. "I did it."

His eyebrow rose a little higher, but he didn't move. "Really? What is it that you did?" Toby didn't really look like the murdering type, but who knew? Baby Chainsaw Killer?

The story came out in halting sentences but was eventually pieced together into something coherent. "I saw her, and I thought it would be, you know, funny, if I, you know, painted her face."

"You put the lipstick on her?"

Toby nodded, still hanging his head. "Yeah. I thought she was passed out. Honest, officer."

"Why passed out?"

Toby looked up, for the first time showing signs of the true eight year old. "Everybody knows she drinks. We seen her pass out at her desk loads of times."

"'We've seen'," the bulldozer corrected sharply.

"Yeah, `we've seen' her passed out plenty of times."

"I don't know why he makes up things like that, officer. I'm sure Miss Gibney did nothing of the sort."

His eyes met the kid's, telling him that he believed him. "That's okay, ma'am. Do you mind if I ask Toby a couple more questions privately?"

"Not at all. Get him to tell you the truth, officer. A good scare is what he needs. Now, Toby, I better not hear that you were giving the officer a bad time. You tell him everything he wants to know, do you understand? Honestly, a child of mine..." She filtered out and he closed the door behind her.

He sat back down. "Do you mind if I ask you a few more questions?"

"No, sir," the kid said, warming to the conversation.

"Good. So, how did you happen to come across Miss Gibney that night?"

"Are you gonna tell my mom?"

"Not if I don't have to."

"It's the best I'm gonna get out of a cop," the kid sighed. "My friends and I sneak out sometimes, you know, after we're supposed to be in bed. We play Dare. You know, dare each other to do stuff. That night, Kenny dared me to get into the school basement. He's kind of a jerk, but I didn't want to look like a chicken," he shrugged his shoulders.

Ah, the terrible realities of the playground. He wondered if Kenny and Toby were headed to a couple of B&E raps later in life.

"...Some kid broke one of the basement windows a few weeks ago. I knew Kenny had been eyeing it. He talked about it couple of times, so I shoulda known he had something in mind. Anyhow, we got in that way."

"This is real important, Toby. What did you see when you got in?"

The kid considered it for a minute. "Not much. It was kind of creepy. I wanted to get out of there right away, but Kenny said no. He wanted to do some exploring, said we'd never get another chance like that." He chuckled. "He just about peed his pants when he saw Carl."

"You mean the janitor?"

"Yeah. Kenny fell over his legs. Scared me pretty bad too. I started running."

"What did Kenny do?"

"At first, I thought he was behind me, but when I looked back, he was just standing there laughing, so I came back."

"What happened then?"

"Carl was snoring so we knew he was just sleeping. We looked around and found his bottles and then we saw Miss Gibney. We figured she was sleeping, too, and Kenny said it'd be a good time to get even with her."

"Even with her for what?"

"You're not gonna tell my mom, are you? She'll be real mad. She thinks teachers are always right." The kid looked scared. He'd probably gotten a beating or two from notes sent home by the old battleaxe. He'd gotten a few of his own and remembered that gut-wrenching fear as you waited for the old man to get home to deliver them.

"I'll try not to, okay. Now what did Miss Gibney do to you?"

"It was after lunch and we were supposed to be doing our math problems. We always do that after lunch because Miss Gibney wants it quiet. She passed out like usual and Kenny and I were whispering, not loud or anything. I needed help with one of the problems. Well, she woke up and was real mad, maddest I've seen her. She slapped Kenny across the face and made him sit under her desk, then she grabbed my arm real hard. Miss Gibney had real long fingernails and whenever she grabbed you, she dug `em in. I started crying. She locked me in the broom closet for the rest of the day. I begged her to let me out. I had to go to the bathroom real bad, but she wouldn't. I ended up peeing my pants. She must've forgot me or something when school was over. I knew it was getting dark out `cause there wasn't any light coming in under the door and I started yelling. Carl heard me and let me out. I had to walk home in pee pants and, boy, was my mom mad at me."

His stomach tightened. Yeah, he remembered moments like that, too. His father's idea of making a man out of him by sending him to military school and you couldn't tell the truth because things would be even worse if you did.

"So you decided to write all over her with lipstick."

"Yeah. I know I shouldn't have."

"It's okay, Toby. I get it. Where did you get the lipstick from."

"We took it out of her purse. Her room was open and, you know, it was funny because when we went in, all the first aid kits were open. The iodine bottles were all out. Kenny and I figured we'd all get in trouble the next day if Miss Gibney saw that mess, so we put everything back together."

A chill ran down his back. Those two kids were probably in the building with the murderer. Thank God, they didn't get hurt, but somebody knew they were there. That wasn't good.

"I want you to tell me something, and it's very important that you tell me the truth about this. Did you do anything else to Miss Gibney?"

"*I* didn't," he said slowly.

"Did Kenny?"

Toby got a little red. "He pulled up her skirts. He thought it would be funny. I thought it was gross."

He sat thoughtfully for a few moments mulling it over.

"Is there anything else you can tell me? Did you see anybody else? Hear anything?"

Toby frowned, pressing his finger thoughtfully against his chin.

"Nope. Just the principal's car leaving."

CHAPTER EIGHT

The voice on the other end of the phone wasn't telling him what he wanted to hear.

"The alternator's on order. Should be in by Friday. Sorry, buddy. Jeb says you can use one of the cars on the lot, though."

"Okay, thanks."

He arranged with the guy to drop off a car to him and by the time he'd eaten the tuna sandwich Ford had brought him from the diner, there was a shiny new cherry red Buick Invicta sitting outside the station. He'd say this much for Jeb, he knew how to take care of his friends. Or maybe he was just a really good salesman. He had to admit, if he was in the market for a car, he'd be tempted. After putting Chuck in charge of getting everything from the lockbox booked into evidence, he slid behind the wheel and started the engine. Purred like a kitten. Yup. He could definitely see this as a possibility. He pulled out of the parking spot and turned right at the light, then hooked a left at the next.

Carl Weaver lived near the end of Fox Street. The brown asphalt shingled house sagged a little in the middle, like it was tired. His shift at the school didn't begin until three, right before the kids were let out. According to Ford, Weaver wasn't married so when an unshaven guy with bleary red-rimmed eyes answered the door, he wasn't surprised.

He gave him the usual spiel and Weaver let him in.

"Want some coffee?" the guy asked as he scuffed his way back to the kitchen. Overall, it was pretty clean for a bachelor's place.

"Thanks." He accepted the cup and took a sip. Not bad.

Weaver leaned against the counter drinking his own cup. "So, you're probably here about Miss Gibney. Thought you'd be coming around sooner or later. I don't have a lot to tell you. I was asleep."

He put his cup on the kitchen table. "Maybe passed out?"

Weaver didn't bat an eye. "Yeah. More like it."

He nodded. "What do you know about what happened that night?"

Weaver thought for a moment. "You know, I've been thinking about it. Tried to remember, but there's not much. I'm a drunk. I tend to not notice an awful lot. That's why I drink. I don't want to notice anything. The only thing I really remember is stumbling up the stairs and coming home to bed."

"You didn't see her?"

"No. That cellar's big, mister. There could be ten bodies down there and in the dark, drunk, I could miss `em all."

Weaver was right. If he was passed out on the other side of the furnace, he could've easily gone upstairs without seeing her.

"Did she ever come down there other times?"

He gave sort of a half-laugh. "Once in a while. She and I, we had an arrangement, you might say. I took care of her bottles and she'd buy some of mine. She kept them in her desk drawer. Every night I'd get them out and once week, I'd go to the liquor store to pick one up for me. She added mine onto her tab there."

"So she had no reason to come down to the cellar?"

"She didn't have any reason to come to see me. Like I said, our arrangement ran like clockwork."

"Can you think of any reason why she went down there that night?"

"The only reason I can think of is if she ran out of booze and wanted some of mine. She knew where I kept it."

"One more question. Did Miss Gibney try to blackmail you?"

There was that half smile again. "Mister, you gotta be afraid of losing something in order for somebody to blackmail you. I haven't got anything left to lose. You know, I started out pretty good. You won't believe it, but I went to Syracuse. Got myself a degree in engineering. Got married, then got shipped off to Korea. They sent me home with a shattered femur. Couldn't walk for a year. The VA put me on pain killers, turned me into a junkie. By the time I kicked that, my wife had run off with a guy she met working at the A&P. You know, after the war, she was the only thing I really cared about. Took up the bottle after that. It's my one vice. I work nights, do my job and don't see nobody. I'm what the VA calls a `functioning alcoholic'. Well, there it is. You don't have to dig for anything on me, mister. It's all right there in the open."

"I'm sorry. You got some tough breaks."

Weaver shrugged. "Everybody gets tough breaks. Some got more than me. I just decided to drink. It makes me invisible. Nobody wants to look at a drunk."

He nodded. Yeah. He understood that. "So what time did you leave?"

"Around eleven. The usual time."

"Did you see anyone when you were leaving?"

He thought for a moment. "Now that you mention it, there was somebody, but I don't know who it was. Just saw the back of 'em going out the door."

"Man or woman?"

"A woman, at least I think so. I just thought it was one of the teachers working late. You know," he paused for a second, "I'm not surprised this happened."

"Why's that?"

"She was losing it. I mean, on the downward spiral, hallucinating, you know."

"How do you know that?"

"Drunks ramble, they all do. Well, one afternoon, a few weeks ago, I was just starting work and went in her room to get the garbage. She looked real confused, more than usual at that time of day. She started rambling on about not wanting to go home because there were people there. I figured, `oh, no, she's gone over the bend now'."

"She tell you who those people might be?"

"She might've, but I couldn't make any sense out of it. It switched from a guy to a woman. Somebody in one of the bedrooms, somebody down cellar. I figured it was just drunk talk."

"Okay. Well, thanks, man. If you think of anything else, give me a call."

Weaver saluted him with his coffee cup. "Will do, chief."

He went down the wooden steps feeling like he'd just talked to the most honest guy on the planet. He looked at his watch. It was nearly three. School would be getting out soon. Grant Stone had a little explaining to do.

A flustered Phyllis Flood was the first person he ran into at the school. She was still shoving her arms into her coat halfway down the main hall.

"Oh, Agent DiPaulo, I, uh," she threw a glance towards the closed door of the principal's office as she adjusted her coat. "Uh, you can't see Mr. Stone right now. He's...busy."

"Thanks, Mrs. Flood, I think he'll find time for me."

"But, Agent DiPaulo," she called after him as he strode down the hall.

Angry voices came out of the principal's office and he glanced back at the secretary who was standing in the middle of the hall with a sick look on her face. After a moment, she scurried off. He turned back to the closed door and listened.

"How long did you think you could keep it a secret. Now that...that dimestore detective probably knows. What are you going to do about it?" It was Mildred Stone's voice.

"Dimestore detective"? Interesting. Made him sound a little like Philip Marlowe. He could live with that.

The principal's voice was hushed. He sounded beaten. "Nothing. There's nothing I can do. It was all done a long time ago."

"So you intend to let our daughter go on like this?"

"What else can we do? Tell her? Do you want to be the one to do that? To destroy her life?"

"Her life? And what about mine? Has it ever occurred to you that this affects my life? What am I supposed to do when that man tells the entire town?" He cringed at the screeching. It reminded him of some of his mother's society friends.

"Agent DiPaulo isn't one of your bridge club members," Stone countered. "He doesn't go blathering gossip all over the place."

She snorted. "Really? And how would you know? I suppose you're great friends with him by now. Yes, that would make sense. He's just the type you would make friends with. Low. Common. If it weren't for me, you'd probably be bringing him and that slut he was seeing home for dinner. Honestly, Grant if it weren't for me, we'd have no standing left in this town."

There was silence. He'd heard gauntlets like that thrown down before and was pretty sure what the outcome would be.

Stone's reply was calm, like the storm in his soul had broken and passed. "I suppose so, Mildred," he said slowly. "It's a good thing you won't have to worry about it anymore."

"What do you mean?"

"I mean I'm leaving you. I'm done. "

She laughed. It wasn't a pleasant sound. "Don't be ridiculous."

"Take it however you want, Mildred, but I'm through."

"You walk out on me and you'll never be superintendent. I'll see to that."

"You and Jeb Sr.?"

"Jeb has nothing to do with this."

There was a sound of disgust. "Jeb's money does. Well, he can keep it. I can live without the promotion."

"You've never understood how things really work. I suppose you think you'll just float off to that little whore you've been screwing. Well, I won't let you."

"You have nothing to say about it."

"You won't get one dime of my family's money."

He heard footsteps coming towards the door. "I don't want your money, Mildred. After twenty-five years of hell, I don't want anything from you."

He slipped back into a nearby alcove as Stone came out, quickly followed by his wife. "You'll regret this, Grant," she threatened.

Stone didn't turn around. Mildred went back into the office and a few moments later left with her coat and purse. The lines of her heavily powdered middle-aged face were hard. He stayed in the shadows until he was sure they were gone.

"Well, thanks for talking with me, Mr. Stone," he said into the darkened hall.

So Grant Stone had a piece of tail on the side. Made sense. A guy like that didn't just leave his wife because he was fed up. They usually suffered in silence until they finally just faded away. Unless, of course, they had something on the side. Between Weaver and the kid, a man and a woman had been seen leaving the school late the night of the murder. Time to find out who Grant Stone was screwing. His jaw tightened. If Mildred knew about it, odds were that Gibney did too. Maybe Grant and his girlfriend decided to do something about it. That is, if she was the one taking the photos.

Benning's was just down the street. He stopped there on the way back to the station. Might be a long night. He settled onto a bar stool. As always, Ralph greeted him like a long lost favorite.

"Starting early, Agent DiPaulo?"

"Nope. Just grabbing some grub to take back to the station."

"What'll ya have?" His hand moved the white bar towel lovingly along the polished oak. "Ann's making up a batch of chicken right now if you're in the mood."

"Sounds good. Give me a couple of pieces and some fries."

"You got it, chief."

Ralph went out back to give his wife the order and he glanced over to the TV. Hotheads were still threatening blacks over those little girls getting enrolled in an elementary school the day before. Eisenhower was all excited about the warheads on our first mobile nuclear site. He'd put in a call to Johnson that morning to find out if there was any local chatter. So far, nothing, but that didn't mean anything. With nukes on the table, things were bound to hot up soon enough. That little bald-headed Khrushchev would never let the US have the upper hand without some sort of show of power. Kennedy was walking into a mess. Maybe he'd do okay. With an old man like his, he probably knew a little something about making deals with thugs.

Ralph came out. "It'll be ready in a couple of minutes. Want something while ya wait?"

"Just coffee. Thanks."

Ralph poured a cup of coffee and put cream and sugar in front of him. He doctored his joe and took a sip. Ralph made some good coffee.

"Ralph," he said, "what d'ya hear about Grant Stone?"

Ralph's eyebrows rose. "Grant? Nothing. He's about as squeaky clean as they come."

"Hmm. That's what I thought."

Ralph leaned forward a little. "For my money, the only thing wrong with Grant Stone is his wife. How such a nice guy ended up with somebody like that, well, it had to be the money. It's what gets a lot 'em in the end."

He sipped more of the coffee. "Tell me about her."

Ralph sipped some of his own coffee and leaned against the bar. "Never liked her. Nobody did. Nasty." Ralph leaned down closer. "I don't usually say this kind of thing, not good for business, but she's a real bitch. Always has been. Her family had money, old money, but she's from Owego, not Park Avenue." He shrugged. "I was a couple of years ahead of her in school. I still remember when she had a "coming out" ball. I got wrangled into being one of the escorts. Never forget it. She walked around like she was the Queen of Sheba. And, believe me, she wasn't anything special to look at, even then."

"So how did she and Grant get together?"

Ralph sipped some more coffee. "Sort of a merger, I'd say. Old man Armstrong, Mildred's father, figured Grant was the best deal his daughter was likely to get. He pulled some strings and got Grant into Harvard with a scholarship. Next thing you know, Grant and Mildred are married. Had to pay his debt, I guess. Poor schmuck never knew what he was walking into"

"What'd he expect? That's how things work. You always gotta pay the piper."

"Yeah. Guys like you and I know that, but Grant wasn't like that. He's one of those true blue guys, maybe too naive. I think he figured he really just got into an Ivy League school because of his smarts. I can just about imagine his face when that old man laid it out for him. Too bad, too. He was going steady with some girl right before all of that happened. Real crazy about her. We all thought they'd end up getting married." He paused a minute, thinking. "Now, who was it? Just a second. Ann," he called out back.

Ann popped her head out of the kitchen. "What?"

"Who was Grant Stone going out with before he went off to Harvard?"

"Oh my gosh, that's ancient history. You know, Ralph. Delphine, remember?"

"Oh my gosh, that's right. Shoulda remembered that. Kind of funny that Delphine ended up working at the school. I guess maybe Grant helped her get the job. Probably felt sorry for her."

"Why?"

Ralph's face got serious. "Delphine's husband, Al, is a pretty bad character."

"How?"

"He's a real jerk. You don't ever look at him cross-eyed. Seen Delphine with a black eye more than once. I'd like to pop the guy myself. I don't like that kind of crap."

He nodded. Ann came out from the back with his bag. "Now, everything's nice and hot, Mr. DiPaulo. You enjoy it."

He grinned at her. "Thanks, Ann. Ralph." He peeled a few bills off and put them on the bar, then slid off his seat. "Have a good night, you two."

On a hunch, he decided to take a drive around town. Maybe he'd get lucky and spot where Grant decided to hole up for the night.

Maybe he'd get really lucky and find him with his girlfriend. Monday night, things were quiet around town. Just after five and it was dark. Cars with their windows all rolled up, guys in heavy overcoats, hats over their ears, hunched over the wheels trying to get warm, were coming down off the hill from IBM, headed home to the wife and kids. Newberry's was beginning to shut off their lights. A skinny assistant manager type was locking the front door. A couple were walking down the street towards the Marble Lounge. He squinted. It was Jill's parents, Hank and Rusty. He wondered what they thought about Jill marrying Jeb. He was sure Rusty was happy about it. She probably saw a new car in her future.

He started the car and began to drive. The Invicta turned down Park St. and then onto Front. Just on the off chance, he's see if Grant had gone home after all. He slowed down. Nope. His car wasn't in the driveway. At the end of Front, he turned down William Street and River towards the small section of town known as Canawanna. Middle class bungalows gradually faded to rundown shacks. There were no street lights so it was hard to decipher where he was exactly. It reminded him of an operation he'd been on that had taken him into the backwoods of Georgia. There was a large bump and the pavement changed to rutted dirt road. Somewhere in the shadows, he caught glimpses of trailers behind overgrown bushes and grass. Up ahead, he saw the faint outline of a car and taillights come on. It stopped in front of a trailer.

"Well, how about that."

It was Grant's black sedan. He slowed and cut his lights, waiting to see what was going on. The trailer door opened and a slight figure ran out and got in the passenger side. The brake lights went off and the sedan started moving.

He followed.

The rabbit warren of one lane roads finally came out onto the main road and he knew where he was. Grant turned left and headed out of town. He had a good idea of where they were headed. A couple of miles down the road the car turned into the Sunrise. He pulled onto the side of the road and waited. Grant left the car running and went into the office. A few minutes later he came out, got into the car and drove over to one of the rooms. As he suspected, when Grant opened the door on the other side, a woman got out. What he didn't expect was for Stone to see the woman to the door, unlock it, let her in, give her a quick kiss and leave.

"What the hell?" he muttered.

Grant's car went back into town and pulled into the school parking lot. He waited for the principal to go in before he did likewise. By the time he was standing in the office doorway, Grant was unfolding a blanket.

"Sleeping on the couch?" he asked.

The principal jumped but quickly recovered. "I didn't hear you. How'd you get in?"

"The janitor must've left the door open."

Stone nodded. "Yeah. I assume you have a reason for being here, Agent DiPaulo. What can I do for you?"

"Who's the broad?"

Stone's mouth opened slightly then shut. "I don't know what you mean."

He sat down. "I think Mrs. Flood will probably tell you tomorrow, so I'll just get it over with now. I heard that little exchange with your wife this afternoon."

Stone dropped down into a chair and clasped his hands in front of him. "Mildred isn't...hasn't been...an easy person."

"So, like I said, who's the broad?"

Stone was a man on a precipice. He almost felt sorry for the poor bastard. When he didn't say anything, he plinked him over the edge. He started to rise.

"How about I go knock on room eleven over at the Sunrise? Maybe I'll get some answers there."

That got out a reaction out of him. Stone jumped up. "No. Don't. Don't bother her."

"Then you got something to tell me?"

"I'll tell you whatever you want, just promise not to bother her."

"That ain't how it works, pal, and you know it. But tell me what I need to know and I'll see what I can do."

Stone hesitated.

"Look, I'm going to find out one way or another."

Stone nodded. "I know. The whole town's going to know. I just didn't want it to happen like this. I wanted to give her everything. I wanted to give her everything I should've given her to start with."

He nodded. "Let's just start with who she is."

"Delphine Chalmers. I love her, Agent DiPaulo. It isn't just some cheap affair. We plan on getting married."

"So now that we have that established, were you both here the night Miss Gibney was murdered?"

Stone nodded. "We saw each other after the meet and greet."

"So, I'm assuming that the baby wasn't the only thing Sybil was holding over your head."

He shook his head. "No. She didn't know anything about Del and I. She would've said something."

"Maybe she said something to Delphine."

"No. Del would've told me."

"Would she? Did Delphine know about you and Miss Gibney?"

"No. No one knows about that."

He weighed whether or not to tell him about the lockbox. Grant Stone could be one very cool customer playing them all.

"What time did you and your girlfriend leave here that night?"

"Around eleven. I remember because she was so scared about getting home late to Al."

He nodded. "Al's her husband?"

"He's an animal. I would've had to leave Mildred soon anyway. I couldn't let that bastard do that to her anymore."

Yeah. He needed to cut the crap with Jill, too. He needed to let it go. Like she said, it never really started.

CHAPTER NINE

If he were writing a book about his life, that day would've been titled "The Trouble with Women". It started right from the get-go. Jill strode into his office at nine sharp. Like every time he'd ever seen her, she made his brain go blank for a few seconds. He could just look at her, in awe of how gorgeous she was.

She dropped his keys on his desk. "Your car's fixed. Jeb wanted me to drop it off for you."

"Thanks."

She waited for a moment and he realized she was waiting for him to hand over the keys to the Invicta. He reached in his pocket and pulled them out.

"Well, have a nice day," she said after taking them and turned to leave.

He racked his brain to think of something to keep her there. "How's your hand?"

She turned back, her green eyes narrowing slightly. "Fine." She held up her hand. The bandage was smaller.

"You didn't need stitches." Well, *that* sounded stupid.

"No. Is that all?"

He held out a chair. "Have a seat. I need your help."

A dubious look swept across her face. "Aren't you supposed to be the detective?"

"This is something you'd know."

She gave a little laugh and sat down. "Sounds serious How's Struble doing, by the way? Coming back soon?"

"You want me gone pretty badly, don't you?"

She crossed her long legs. "I think you know the answer to that."

He shut the door. "They're letting him out today. He'll be back at work next week. I wanted to ask you about this."

"Okay. Shoot. I'm in a hurry."

"Your baby, how would you find it?"

"Wow, you don't pull any punches, do you?"

"I'm sorry. I shouldn't have asked. It was stupid."

"No. It's all right. It's something I did. I made the decision."

"No, I'm sorry. I don't know what I was thinking. Guys are stupid sometimes."

She gave a half-smile. "Yeah, I know. Look, you can't find your kid after you give it up."

"What do you mean? You mean never?"

"Yeah, never. It's to protect the kid."

He thought a moment, rubbing his chin. "What if the kid grew up and wanted to find you?"

"They couldn't, well, maybe with a private detective or something, I guess. Why are you asking me this? Does this have something to do with that teacher dying?"

He hesitated. "Yeah."

"Oh. Well, I hope I helped you out."

"You did. Thank you."

They were looking into each other's eyes. He wanted her to stay because when she walked out that door again it might be the last time he ever saw her. He didn't want that.

The door opened and a very stylish silver-haired woman entered.

"I'm here to let you take me to lunch for my birthday," she said, and then, "Am I interrupting?"

"Mom? What are you doing here?"

"I believe I've already stated my purpose," and then to Jill, "Hello."

He tried to recover his shock. "Uh, this is Miss Kaufman. Jill, this is my mother."

Jill got up and held out her hand. "Mrs. DiPaulo."

"Miss Kaufman, very nice to meet you. I hope I'm not interrupting anything important."

His mother turned on her dazzling smile, the one she always used when meeting someone important for the first time. That should've been his first inkling of what was to come.

Jill adjusted her fur. Seeing the two of them in the same room, he was surprised at how similar they were. For some reason, Jill reminded him of a younger version of his mother. A little tougher perhaps, but with just as much class. A stupid thought ran across his brain and he wondered if they'd be friends or rivals if Jill was her daughter-in-law. Idiot.

"I was just leaving," Jill replied. "It's very nice to meet you, Mrs. DiPaulo. Agent DiPaulo." The cool, untouchable mask as back in place.

"Thanks, Miss Kaufman. We'll be in touch."

She nodded but said nothing and left.

"What a beautiful girl. I'm not surprised you never made it this weekend," she ran a gloved finger along the edge of his desk and sat down.

"My car really did break down."

She grinned. "It's sitting outside."

"She just brought it back. It was in her fiancé's garage."

Her brow rose. "So they send girls in fur coats to deliver cars around here? Interesting. Small town life is a little different than I thought it would be."

"She's a friend, mom."

"Umhmm. Take me to lunch and you can tell me all about her."

What did you say when your mother travels six hours to have lunch with you? He got his coat and took her to lunch.

Ralph hadn't even put their drinks in front of them before she started in on him. "Why are you letting that gorgeous girl marry someone else?"

"Can we at least give our orders first?"

Ralph came over and smiled between the two of them. "Hey, Agent DiPaulo, what can I get for you and the lovely lady?"

"Ralph, this is my mother, Mrs. DiPaulo. Mom, this is Ralph Benning. He keeps me fed."

She shook his hand. "Thank you, Mr. Benning, for taking such good care of my boy." She leaned forward, "Now, what would you suggest for lunch?"

Oh, his mother was charming. Ralph was grinning all over himself. They placed their orders and as soon as Ralph went off, his mother started in on him again.

"Well?" she said.

"There's a lot of gorgeous women in the world, mom."

She gave a ladylike little snort. "Not ones that are in love with you. And before you tell me I'm crazy, I already know there's something going on. You didn't just tell your father that you were coming into the bank without something serious going on and if I know my son that involves a woman."

"I think we need you in the agency."

"So, I state my question again. Why are you letting her marry another man?"

"If you want to know the truth, she doesn't want anything to do with me."

She tsked and took a sip of the Beefeater's martini that Ralph had put in front of her. "Nonsense."

"Look, mom, I saw her a few times. Things happened. It's over."

"*Things happened*? Like you took her to bed."

Nothing like discussing your sex life with your mother. "Geez, mom."

"Oh, for goodness sake. You think I don't know what goes on between men and women."

"Guys don't talk about sex with their mothers."

She laughed. "I think you're blushing. Well, I'm the one with the birthday. We'll talk about what I want to talk about."

"Olaf drove you," he grumbled.

"Irregardless, I'm the one who came here. We're going to have a lovely lunch, I'm going to treat myself to two martinis, and I'm going to find out why you're thinking about walking away from what you love to do."

His mother sure as hell didn't need to know about Ben Samuels and his sister-in-law. "I just realized it was the best thing."

She ate the olive. "You must be crazy about her." She reached over and put her hand on top of his. "Marry her. Stay with the agency. Be happy. Don't end up like your father." Ralph put their Reubens in front of them. She smiled. "Now, let's eat."

His mother was staying at the Regency in Binghamton that night and then going onto the city the next day for a little shopping. He tucked her into her Cadillac later that afternoon knowing in no uncertain terms that if he didn't do what she said, he'd never live it down. Great. At least she liked the gifts he'd gotten her.

It wasn't over. Oh, no. He was in for another treat.

He entered Struble's office with the intention of barricading the door and going through the contents of the lockbox with a fine tooth comb. Nope. Another woman to contend with. This one looked scared.

"Agent DiPaulo?" she turned in her chair as he opened the door.

"Yes?"

"I'm Delphine Chalmers. I think you might want to talk to me."

He took his chair behind the desk and leaned back. His eyebrow rose. "I think you're right, Mrs. Chalmers, and just for the record, where were you the night Sybil Gibney was murdered?"

She bit her lip. One of those fragile women who still had the vestiges of a youth long past. He could see why Stone would leave his wife for her. She seemed sweet and warm and understanding, a breath of fresh air after that battleaxe he was married to. It didn't mean she couldn't snap and do something stupid. Or maybe Stone talked her into helping him get rid of a problem. Either way, there were a lot of sweet women who did some pretty awful things and poison was a woman's game.

"I was at the school. We...I...must've been there when she was murdered, but I didn't do it. I swear. I'm telling you all the truth. Here, I even brought this to show you I have nothing to hide. All my secrets are in there." She put a shoebox on his desk in front of him. "Go ahead, open it."

He lifted the top. Inside were the same type of things he'd seen in the lockbox. He picked up the pictures and looked closely. Her and Grant Stone. At least that was one mystery solved. When he looked back at her, she'd turned red.

"I'd find these in my locker," she explained. "It started a little while after Grant and I..."

She left it hanging and he finished it for her. "Starting seeing each other. So who put these there?"

"I don't know, but I'm afraid. Maybe it's the same person who killed Sybil. I've wondered that ever since. I'm afraid someone will kill me too."

Tears started running down her face and she pulled a handkerchief out of her bag.

"I'm sorry. I'm just so scared. If Al finds out, if he even finds me, he'll kill me. I was terrified every time I found these. I knew someone was watching us. Mr. DiPaulo, please, I'm scared. Can you please help me?"

"Did you kill Sybil Gibney?"

She looked like someone had thrown a bucket of cold water on her. "No. No. I wouldn't. Why? Why would I do something like that?"

"Because Sybil Gibney was probably the one leaving those things in your locker. Maybe you just decided you'd had enough."

He had his answer. There was a look of utter relief on her face.

"Really? Was it really her? Oh, thank God," she said with a shaky smile.

"I think so. So, did Grant know about this stuff?"

"No. I never told him. I didn't want to worry him more than he already was."

"Why was Mr. Stone so worried?"

"Leaving his wife. He knew, we both knew, what it would mean for his career. And there was Al."

"What about Al?"

She undid the top buttons of her blouse and pulled it open just enough for him to see the bruises.

He nodded. "Your husband did that? He knew about you and Stone?"

She buttoned her blouse. "He knew there was someone. I don't think he knew for sure who it was."

"You know, I saw Grant take you to the Sunrise last night. If I found you, your husband can probably find you too. I mean, there's only two motels in town."

She bit her lip again. "I know. We didn't know what else to do. Grant called me yesterday afternoon and told me that he'd left his wife and that he wasn't going to let me stay with Al any more. He told me to go to a friend's house and he'd pick me up there so that Al wouldn't know."

"So that place in Canawanna was where your friend lives?"

"How did you know about that?"

"I was out looking for Stone. It was just good luck. The point is, you need someplace safe to stay. Got any relatives, friends you could stay with?"

"No place Al wouldn't go looking for me."

"Maybe I know a place."

He picked up the receiver, his fingers hesitating before finally dialing the number.

"Hello, Jill?"

He checked to see if Al Chalmers had gone to work that day and then had Ford take Delphine over to Jill's. It was better that he didn't go. Instead, he went to Binghamton. It was way past time that he checked on things there. He owed Moriarty that much.

"Well, long time no see. How's the bigshot?" Johnson said as he came through the door.

"Haha. Very funny." He reached in the paper bag he was carrying and threw a sandwich to the agent. "How deep is the pile?"

Johnson unwrapped the waxed paper and lifted the edge of the bread. "Tuna. Not bad. I forged your signature on a few requisition forms. The boys and I thought it'd be nice to have a poker table."

He went into Moriarty's office and flipped on the light. "You're a real laugh riot, Johnson. Maybe you oughtta be on the Tonight Show."

Johnson laughed and chewed a bite of his sandwich. "Yeah. I'd be good. So, how's things in little old Owego? Hoppin' little place from what I hear."

"It sees its fair share of action. Where's the files on the Jablonski kidnapping?"

"Over there. I got statements from everybody. No ransom demands yet. It's not looking very good for the kid. I put Flaherty and Nebraska on it, just like you said."

"Thanks."

Johnson filtered out and he buried himself in the files on Morarty's desk. Susan Jablonksi was a thirteen year old Binghamton girl out delivering the evening paper when she disappeared. No trace of her. They'd checked all her friends, relatives, customers, everybody. Nothing except a light colored Fairlane. It kept hitting him again and again how tragic it was. That kid was probably dead. As dead as Sybil Gibney. There were a lot of people who were going to be devastated when that little girl's body was found. It seemed like a real waste of time looking for Sybil Gibney's murderer. Nobody gave a shit about her. In fact, the world was probably a better place without her. But there it was, that was the nature of the beast.

Johnson was long gone when he realized how late it was. He looked at the clock. Quarter to nine. He should stop in to see Moriarty.

The hospital was quiet when he got there, most everybody tucked in for the night. The nurses sat at their stations with little lamps on, the hallways dim. It wasn't like they let anybody sleep anyway. Always going in to take your blood pressure or jab you with a needle.

When he asked to see his boss, the night nurse looked over her glasses at him and then at the clock. "It's late. You gentlemen should've been gone hours ago. Really, I don't know how you expect him to get any better."

"Gentlemen?"

"The other man. I told him to leave five minutes ago."

He didn't like the feeling he was getting. "How about I go remind the guy. I'll just look in on Mr. Moriarty and be right out, I promise."

She looked at him skeptically.

"You know as well as I do that he's not getting any better," he reasoned.

She nodded. "Just be out in five minutes."

He thanked her and headed down the hall. As he got closer, he heard muted voices coming from the room. He stopped short and listened for a moment. Immediately, he knew why he'd gotten a bad feeling.

Ben Samuels was talking. "... You're dying. Face it. You can't just leave this stuff laying around. It's bigger than you and I."

Moriarty coughed. "It's not laying around." His voice was gravelly, barely above a whisper, but he could hear the derision in it.

He edged closer and looked in. Samuels faced away from him, but his body was tense. He knew how angry he was. He'd heard that tone before, but there was a little something more to it now. There was a touch of anxiety.

"You son-of-a-bitch, give them to me," Samuels demanded. "It's time. You've wrung enough out of me."

"And I'm going to wring a lot more. You're late with a payment. I want it. Now." He could just see Moriarty's face. His boss was dead serious. His face didn't look sick now. He looked just as tough as any street hood.

Samuels gave an ugly laugh. "Yeah. I'll just do that." Before Moriarty could say another word, he grabbed the pillow under his head and leaned over.

Son-of-a-bitch was going to kill him. He walked in, loudly as he could. "Old home week," he announced.

Samuels quickly stuffed the pillow back under Moriarty's head, giving it a few pats like he was plumping it up. He wanted to kick that guy's ass in the worst way, but kept his cool.

Samuels looked a little shaken. "Yeah. Just thought I better check in with one of my best men."

He gave Moriarty a nod. "How's things, boss?"

"Not bad. Having a little chat with the director, here. He was just about to give me a little present, weren't you, Mr. Samuels?"

"Yeah. That is, I left it out in the car. I'll, uh, bring it up tomorrow."

Moriarty's eyes bore through the director's. "That'll be great." The threat was plain.

Samuels left soon after.

"You must be a pretty important guy for the director to drive all the way from DC just for a visit," he said.

Moriarty chuckled. "Hand me some water, smart-ass."

He poured some in a cup. The same lukewarm crap. It was useless to ask if he could get him some cold. Moriarty was too much of a tough guy.

"How ya feelin'?" he said as he handed it to him.

"Gettin' better."

"You don't look it."

"A lot you know. Sit down. Tell me about your case."

He pulled the chair over and they talked. He gave him the details, but the whole time, all that ran through his head was the vision of Samuels about to murder a dying man. Things were deep between his boss and the director, deep enough for Samuels to want to take a big risk.

'You got a mystery on your hands, kid. Wish I was up to it."

Moriarty was getting antsy, his hands clenching and unclenching the sheets, raking his fingers through his hair. His skin was paler than before and sweat was beginning to bead on his forehead. It was his eyes that told him how much pain he was in, that, and the clenching of his jaw.

"When do they give you your shot?" he asked. It made him hurt just looking at him.

Moriarty's eyes kept darting to the clock. "Ten. When they're on time."

It was nine-thirty.

"I'll be right back."

Moriarty barely nodded.

He went out to the nurse's station. "You're late," she said not looking up. "I should've kicked you out."

"Yeah, okay," he said, "Look, he needs his shot."

She looked at her watch. "It's not time," she said and went back to her ledger.

"He needs it."

"I'm sorry, sir, we have to stick to the schedule. Morphine is highly addictive. You don't want him to get addicted, do you?"

It took some doing to keep him from pulling her out of that chair and marching her white polyester covered ass down the hall to his friend, but he didn't. "That guy's dying. He needs a shot. Who gives a damn if he turns into a junkie?"

The anger in his voice got her attention, but only slightly. She looked up at him. "Sir, really, you won't be helping him."

It was the bored, dismissive tone that sent him over the edge. He grabbed the clipboard out of her hand. "Look, sister, either you do it or I do. And don't think I don't know what I'm doing. I've seen more junkies that you ever will."

Her jaw tightened and whatever claim she might've had to pretty faded quick. "I'm calling security." She reached for the phone.

"You pick up that phone and I'll make sure you never work again. Got it?"

She hesitated with her hand over the phone for a second.

"Your choice, sister. You pick up that phone and I go make my own phone call." He wasn't entirely sure who he'd call, but he'd figure it out. The important thing was that she bought his bluff.

She tsked and gave him a dirty look as she got up and began to unlock the medicine cupboard. "Fine. You're the boss, but you're doing him more harm than good. It'll just be a longer wait until the next shot."

She readied the tray and he was sure that she took her time with it, just to piss him off. It was working.

The lines of Moriarty's face eased as soon as she jammed it into his arm and it wasn't long before he was sleeping. The nurse left and he stayed.

"You're a good guy, Moriarty," he said to the still room. "Wish you didn't have to go this way."

As much as he'd wanted to avoid coming in there before, now he was reluctant to leave. He couldn't shake the feeling that this was going to be the last time he'd see him. It made him feel like shit.

He took Moriarty's hand and gave it a squeeze. "It's been good to know you, buddy."

On the way out, he stopped by the nurse's station. "You know he's dying, right?"

She met his eyes, her own expression stony, not giving an inch, but he saw in her eyes that she knew.

"Just give him his shot when he needs it, will ya?"

Her voice softened slightly. "Look. I know it's hard seeing your friend like this, and I wish I could help him out, but there are rules. If I get caught breaking them, I could be arrested."

He nodded. That left it up to him. "When is he supposed to get his shots?"

"Every four hours."

"Okay. See you tomorrow." He began to walk away.

"Hey," she called, "Don't do anything stupid."

"I won't."

Sid Lau ran a high class Chinese restaurant in the middle of Binghamton. He was also a purveyor of whores. His path had run across Sid's when the whores' abortionist had gotten sucked into his last investigation. That guy had gotten sloppy and ended up in jail. Maybe the next one would be a little more conscientious. As usual, Sid's restaurant was in full swing when he went through the doors. The Chinese doorman recognized him and gave him that buck-toothed smile. "Ah, Mr. DiPaulo, table for one?"

"I need to see Mr. Lau."

He dropped the grin. "Mr. Lau know you coming?"

"No. It's a spur of the moment visit, but I think he'll want to see me."

The guy nodded. "I go see. Wait here."

A waitress passed, her scarlet silk dragon embroidered sheath tight across her ass as she gave him the eye. Those cool, appraising Asian eyes signaled dangerous, exotic sex and he wondered if her full-time job was upstairs. Her hips undulated to one of the tables. As long as he had to wait, he could appreciate the long slit in her skirt that showed thigh almost to the round cleft of her rear as she bent to serve drinks. An inspiring sight.

A few minutes later, smiling boy returned and led him back through the noisy kitchen to Lau's office. The door closed behind him leaving the steam and chaos outside. Sid rose to greet him.

"To what do I owe this honor, Agent DiPaulo?"

"I need some help and I thought you might be just the guy."

"What can I do for you?"

"I need a doctor."

Sid's brows rose above his glasses for a moment, then he chuckled and he held up his hands. "I run a restaurant, not a hospital."

He leaned forward. "I prefer not to bring up your other business activities, but I will if I need to," he said softly.

"We needn't go into such details."

"Good. I'm assuming you got somebody to replace Adams. I'll make it worth his while to do me a favor."

"If I may ask, what is the favor?"

"I have a friend dying of cancer. He needs morphine."

Lau sat back in his chair. "That's a very big favor, Agent DiPaulo. You realize the implications of such a request."

And then it hit him what the implications were. Sid Lau would have something on him for life. He'd end up a dirty cop. He might be a cop that cut some corners when it was necessary, but he wasn't about to hand a pimp his balls.

He began to rise. "You know, Mr. Lau, you got a point, there. I guess I just lost it for a little bit. Sorry to have bothered you."

Sid held out his hand. "No bother, Agent DiPaulo. We all lose our way one time or another."

If anybody knew, it would be Sid Lau.

His mind was in turmoil all the way back to Owego. It was after eleven by the time he drove down Main Street. He slid into a parking slot in from of Benning's.

It was a week night and the bar was empty except for Ralph. He was in the process of closing up.

"Out late tonight, Agent DiPaulo," he said as he put a coaster in front of him.

"Didn't feel like going home right away. Give me a draft."

"You're the boss."

Ralph poured a beer and set it in front of him.

"Seem a little troubled tonight. Everything okay with your mother?"

He waved a hand and let about half the cold, smooth beer slide down his throat. "She's fine. Probably sleeping like a baby right now."

Ralph grinned. "Nice lady."

"Yeah, she is. Wants me to get married."

Ralph chuckled. "They all do," he said diplomatically. "Anyone in particular?"

"Who do you think?"

Ralph nodded. "Yeah. That's tough." He rubbed his chin. "I thought Jill really liked you, too."

He set his empty glass down and tapped the coaster. Ralph poured another.

"Yeah, well, guess I'm not the ladies man I thought I was. Or the one my mother thought I was, anyhow."

"Women. You know, I don't give advice, but I got observations. Sometimes men gotta lay it out for women. Women want to know where they stand. If they don't, well," he shrugged his shoulders. "they jump to conclusions. Usually the wrong ones. Like I said, just an observation."

"Yeah. You're probably right." He finished the last of his beer, paid up and left.

It was cold out. A few flakes of snow drifted down, just enough to tell him how cold it was. He went back to Struble's place. Patty must've been by earlier. Everything was spotless, ready for him to come home. He kicked off his shoes and laid down on the couch, pulling a blanket over him. He'd already booked a room at the Sunrise for the next day. Their wedding was the next week.

He shut his eyes and tried to sleep, but couldn't. He kept thinking about Jill walking down that aisle with Jeb Burks. If he tried to switch gears, he ended up thinking about Moriarty laying there dying. Shit. What a night.

CHAPTER TEN

Chuck came in the office all grins that morning. "Have I got something for you, boss."

The sergeant held up a smashed Polaroid camera.

"Where the hell did you find that?"

Chuck set it down on the desk. "Behind the incinerator at the school. Looked like somebody tried to throw it in and missed. It was wedged pretty good in between the incinerator and the fence. It took two of us guys and a crowbar to get it out."

"Well, what d'ya know. How'd you think to look there?"

"I didn't. Some kid was playing around there, caught hell from one of the teachers, and the teacher saw it."

"Nice work, Chuck. Dust it for prints and lock it up."

He went back to sorting through the pictures again. Somewhere inside of them, they told a piece of the puzzle. The pictures that people kept always did. He held up one. It was a young woman of twenty-three or so. An average looking young woman in her straight, boxy 1920's style dress. Maybe a little shy, her arms folded over her chest hugging a school book, her glasses a little askew. If he looked hard enough, he saw the young Sybil Gibney in that girl, a new teacher, before she turned into a drunken old bat. He placed it next to a picture with writing on it stating "Owego Elementary School - June, 1930". It was a group of teachers standing in front of the school. They were all smiling, some squinting a little in the bright summer sunshine. What was striking about the picture was the look on Sybil's face. Her head was turned slightly towards the man standing next to her and it didn't take much of an imagination to see what she felt. Grant Stone faced forward, not noticing the look of adoration on his colleague's face. Young Grant Stone reminded him of Gary Cooper, that clean-cut, chiseled, knight-in-shining-armor thing. He was a man that women fell in love with.

It didn't take a cop to know how much trouble that kind of a guy could stir up.

He flipped through the rest, but nothing stuck in his mind like the look on Sybil's face as she looked at Grant Stone thirty years ago. He set them down and picked up the birth certificate.

Where was that kid now? Had she known him, seen him? Something told him that giving up this kid was the incident that triggered everything leading up to Sybil Gibney's death. He had to go back to her house. Maybe a walk around it would make something click. At the very least, maybe he'd find the camera and clear up at least one mystery.

He grabbed his coat. "I'll be back in a little while, Chuck. Hold down the fort."

"Sure boss."

Dead leaves swirled around his ankles as he stood on the sidewalk looking up at her house. It was a place of sadness, despair. It was a place that had harbored a shy reclusive child who grew into a woman whose unrequited love had ended up in a life-shattering outcome. It was the hidden cave of a normal woman who hadn't had a chance to live a normal life and had turned into a decaying relic as rundown as the house itself. Shakespeare couldn't spin a worse tragedy.

He let himself in. The boys from the agency had done their job, but other than that, nothing seemed different. He went through everything with a fine tooth comb. He sat down at her desk and pulled out the papers. They were neat and in order. Definitely not the usual result of a bunch of flatfoots nosing around. There were three bank accounts. The first two were at the Owego National and had a hundred dollars or so, nothing to write home about. He picked up the third. It was at First City, the Binghamton branch.

He gave a low whistle. "Holy shit." He thumbed through the pages of the savings passbook. Page after page of deposits, years of them. There was over thirty thousand bucks in it. She must've been saving it from the time she started working. He was in for a bigger surprise. The name on the account wasn't Sybil Gibney. It was Alan Carroway.

He sat back just looking down at that name. Alan Carroway. Was he Sybil Gibney's kid? The fight between Stone and his wife made sense now. This was the secret that was going to ruin Mildred Stone's life. It'd never been about his affair. It was about two kids committing incest. Now that was a secret to blow the lid off a small town.

He was about to leave when he heard something overhead. Adrenaline shot through his veins like a fixer's needle. He pulled his revolver out of the shoulder holster he always wore and moved silently up the stairs. It was a rhythmic sound like something rubbing against wood. The doors to all the rooms were closed as he headed down the hallway. A floorboard creaked and he froze, holding his breath, flattening against the wall. The noise stopped for a second, too, as if someone else was waiting, holding their breaths, then it began again, this time faster, more urgent.

It was coming from Sybil's room. Maybe just a couple of kids had sneaked in to make out. He poised himself in front of the door, took a deep breath and kicked it in.

"Shit."

He holstered his gun and went to the bed. On it was a young girl, naked and handcuffed to the headboard. Blood was smeared on her legs and she was crying. Her eyes were terrified and she shrank from him as he went to undo her gag.

"Please, please, don't," she begged, sobbing so hard he could barely make out the words. She was hysterical.

"It's okay, honey," he said, trying to soothe the frightened girl. "I'm a cop and nobody's going to hurt you. I promise. My name is Nick and I'm going to help you." He covered her over with a blanket and looked around for a key. There wasn't anything there.

"Is there anybody else here?"

She shook her head. "Please get me out of here, please."

He looked at the headboard. It was an old-fashioned one, the kind with spindles.

"Honey, I've gotta break this headboard to get you out. Don't be scared."

Using every bit of force he could, he kicked the top of the headboard again and again. Finally, he heard it crack. One last kick and it gave. He pulled the pieces apart, freeing the cuffs. The poor kid's wrists were raw.

"We'll have to get them off at the station," he told her, pulling an old coat out of Sybil's wardrobe and putting it around her.

He helped her up. She was shaky as all get out and he didn't blame her. He recognized her from the picture. Susan Jablonski, the thirteen year old from Binghamton. All he could feel was relief that she'd been found alive.

It was a long night. He called her parents, then took her to the hospital. His jaw tightened while he paced the hallway outside the examining room. It was like the kid was getting raped all over again, having strangers pawing over her, touching her in spots that she couldn't even say without being embarrassed. All he could think of was how he'd feel if that was his daughter. He'd commit murder in a heartbeat. Maybe the good news was that she couldn't tell him much about the man who'd done that to her.

It was late before he'd seen the kid home and finished the initial paperwork. The kid's parents were falling all over themselves thanking him. He didn't feel like much of a hero. You never felt like a hero when you saw stuff like that. It made you sick inside.

He needed a drink and to forget about it for a little while. He needed Jill.

Jeb Senior's house was lit up like Christmas. Music spilled out into the frosty suburban night. A few laughing people came through the front door saying their good nights and laughing. They came down the sidewalk kind of wobbly and obviously filled with good spirits and expensive booze. He wanted to feel like that, too. At least for a few hours, until he had to come back to reality.

He entered the house and was piling his coat on top of the others when he saw her. She was laughing, a glass of champagne in her hand, her body encased in a white shimmery gown. He just wanted to look at her. How was it possible that she was so gorgeous? He felt a hunger for her that he'd tried to make himself forget for a long time. His mother was right. He couldn't let her marry some other guy. He had to have her.

He made his way to her, just as the others faded away.

"Dance with me," he asked.

She set her glass down. "Why not."

They blended in with the others, their bodies melding together, their warmth enveloping them in a place all their own.

"At last, my love has come along..." Etta James crooned from the stereo. He breathed in the scent of her and held her hand close against his chest.

"Marry me, Jill," he whispered. "I need you."

She pulled back a bit and met his eyes. For once there wasn't a wall, they weren't cool and they weren't pushing him away. There was only pain. "Oh, Nick...," she said sadly.

"And life is like a dream...."

And suddenly he understood the white dress, the big party. His arms fell from her. He felt like somebody had just kicked him in the gut. Jeb came up to them and put his arm around her, that big stupid grin on his face.

"Did my girl tell you the big news?" he asked. "Quite a surprise, huh?"

"Yeah," he said, his mouth feeling like sawdust. His eyes never left hers. They were shiny and he wanted to pull her out of there, out of the mistake that they'd both made. Instead, he offered his hand to Jeb. "Congratulations. I hope you'll both be very happy."

"Thanks, Nick. I've got quite a peach here." Jeb kissed her cheek. "Don't mind if I steal my wife for a dance do ya? This is our song. Come on, honey."

Jeb put his arm around her waist and she placed her hand in his. She kept looking at him until they disappeared in the crowd then he turned around and left, so numb he could barely feel his feet. He sat in his car, just staring for a long time before turning on the ignition. Who'd he been kidding anyway?

He was a different man when he walked into the station the next morning. His head had cleared. All the crap had been sorted out. She'd been right a long time ago. They'd never even started. Moriarty would die, somebody would take his place and he'd go into his dad's bank. He'd finish these cases and do what he should've to start with.

He pulled out the girl's statement from the night before, that and the medical reports. Cold detachment settled over him as he read the details. He'd grabbed her as she passed an alley, covering her mouth with a handkerchief that smelled funny. Chloroform. He thumbed through the medical record. There were several needle marks too. He must've kept her knocked out. Somebody that had access to knock-out drugs. That was a wide field, but there was only one person with that kind of background that he could imagine using Sybil Gibney's house for a play den.

He picked up the phone and dialed. A feminine voice answered. "Hello?"

"Mrs. Olkowski?"

"Yes?"

"This is Agent DiPaulo. I have a few questions I'd like to ask. Can I come over?"

There was hesitation. "Can I come there?" she said in a hushed voice.

It didn't take long for her to get there. He ushered her into the office.

"No interruptions, Ford. Nobody."

Ford nodded and he shut the door behind him.

"I want the truth. Was Alan Carroway with you last Saturday afternoon?"

Her eyes lowered and she bit her bottom lip.

"Look, so far, I've played ball with you, but I'm losing patience. Tell me now, or maybe I need to call in Mr. Olkowski and see what he has to say."

"No, he wasn't with me."

"Where was he?"

She shrugged her shoulders. "How would I know?"

"Well, you two seem pretty cozy." He didn't say it nicely. "Okay, where are your girls?"

Her eyes widened. "At school. Why?"

His jaw tightened as he threw a few photos down in front of her, pictures of Susan Jablonski's blood smeared legs, pictures of the handcuffs and beds where she'd been held prisoner. "I want to talk to them. Alone."

She picked up the pictures, looking at them slowly, then looked up at him. "What's this about?"

He took the pictures from her. "I don't want your girls to end up like that. Now, do I have your consent?"

Her face had turned pale. "I want to know what this is about."

It was the way she said it. He played the hunch. "I think you know." He folded his arms over his chest and leaned against the desk. "You know there's something wrong with him."

Her eyes snapped up to his.

"But you can't put your finger on it," he finished.

She looked away from him, but he saw the nod of her head.

"Tell me."

Her tapered red nails picked at the edge of her trench coat. "Nothing really. It's just a feeling. I'm being stupid."

"Why don't you let me be the judge of that. Tell me what didn't sit right with you."

She took in a deep breath. "Hal was out of town for a few nights. A conference or something, I never can keep tract. Anyhow, Alan came over. The girls were in bed, no one was around. After we made love, I must've drifted off. Something woke me up, probably a bad dream or something. I know I was startled. The bed was empty, so I figured Alan had gone off home. I went to check on the girls and..." She bit her lip and stopped.

"And what?"

"Alan was coming out of Barbie's room. He only had his underwear on and he was...hard."

"What did you do?"

"I asked him what was going on."

"And what did he say?"

"He said he heard Barbie crying and didn't want to wake me so he went to check on her."

"And about the hard-on?"

"He said it was just morning wood."

He allowed her own words to sink in for a few moments. "The alarm bells went off."

She nodded. "I tried to tell myself everything was all right. Maybe it really is. I mean, he's a doctor, I've known Alan since we were kids. He wouldn't do anything bad like that."

"Maybe not. Your girls ever complain of being sore down there, any problems, infections or anything?"

"A few times."

"Alan was their doctor?"

She nodded again. "You don't really think he did anything to them do you? I mean it's not like he's a pervert. Look at him, he's a normal, regular guy. He cuts his own grass, for Heaven's sake. Do perverts do that?"

He pushed a paper in front of her and put a pen beside it. "Let me talk to the girls. Let's make sure."

Her hand shook as she signed it.

On the way to the school that afternoon to interview the girls, he drove past Carroway's house. There were several cars parked in front of the house, meaning that he was busy in the office. He stopped down the street and walked up the driveway, careful to avoid any of the windows, and came up alongside the garage. Carroway's car, the one he took the lockbox from was parked in front of it. He shielded his eyes and looked inside the garage.

There, inside, was a cream-colored Fairlane.

"I've got you, you son-of-a-bitch."

When he got to the school, he called Ford and told him to start making out a search warrant. At least the judge couldn't say he was interrupting his game today.

"This would probably be the best place to speak to the girls. Is there anything I can do to help?" Stone asked after he showed him the release Debbie Olkowski signed.

"No. Thanks. Just send them in one at a time."

Stone nodded, his face concerned. Barbie, the older of Debbie Olkowski's little girls, was sent in first. His heart kind of melted. At eight, she still had that baby chubbiness. She was a little princess, with bright blue eyes, pink cheeks, and blonde curls. She sat down in the chair across from him and smiled up at him with her missing front teeth, that innocence, and he hated what he had to do.

He left the school that afternoon, went around back and puked in the bushes. Thank God, he was leaving this crap.

The door to Carroway's office was unlocked, but the receptionist and all the patients were gone. Perfect timing. It was about time something went right.

Carroway was going through his medicine chest. He looked up. "I was just closing up."

"I have a warrant for your records and your Fairlane."

"Sure," Carroway said with a smug, cool smile. "Sorry about that the last time you were here. Guess I'm not used to having cops go through my stuff. It all worked out though." He handed a key to him. "The records are in the filing cabinets by my receptionist's desk. If you don't mind, I'll just finish up here. Gotta inventory every day."

He nodded and went back down the hall to the waiting room. He unlocked the drawers and ran his finger down the labels until her found the "O's". He squatted down and pulled it open. He was about to pull out a file when he realized he wasn't alone. Carroway's arm came down like an axe, the needle in his hand grazing his skin as he grabbed his arm.

"I'm so glad you tried that, you bastard," he growled.

He shoved the doctor backwards. Carroway lost his balance and fell into another cabinet. His hands shot out and he grabbed him by his shirt and pulled him up, his fist ramming into his face, once, twice, three times before the guy had a chance to put up a fight. Carroway tried to push him away, but was too dazed. He pulled his arm up behind his back hard until the doctor cried out.

"You fucking little punk, shut up," he pulled the arm up sharper and Carroway bit his lip and groaned.

He pulled cuffs out of his pocket and shackled the guy's hands behind him, then shoved him into a chair and socked him in the face one more time.

"That was for knocking me out." He flexed his fingers then picked up one of the other chairs and sat down across from him.

"Here's what's going to happen," he said, wiping sweat from his forehead. "You're going to tell me everything I want to know. I'm gonna write it down and you're gonna sign it. You got that?"

Carroway nodded then looked up.

He turned to see Judge Barton standing there with a revolver in his hand. "I don't think we've ever been formally introduced, Agent DiPaulo. I'm Augustus Carroway Barton. Alan is my adopted son. Now hand over that piece you have strapped to your shoulder."

Well, another twist to a case that was starting to look like a maze. Hadn't figured for this one. He pulled the gun from its holster and passed it over.

Barton pocketed the gun. "Now, you're going to unlock his cuffs and we're going for a ride."

He did as he was told. Getting taken out by a corpulent, dirty judge wasn't how he'd pictured leaving this world, but, hey, there were other, worse ways. Once Carroway's wrists were freed, Barton gave him one of the guns.

"Get in the back," Barton told him.

He climbed into the back seat of the two-tone Olds. Barton and his son got in the front.

"So which one of you did it?" he asked as they headed towards the tracks.

"Did what?" Carroway asked. "The girl? Dad didn't have anything to do with that."

"Your real dad or this guy sitting here?" he nodded towards Barton.

"Nobody knows who my real father was. Not even you."

He laughed. "You mean mommy never told you? No, I guess she wouldn't. When did she tell you who she was?"

"I'm not telling you anything," Carroway said.

Barton turned onto Prospect Street. The street was narrow and kids were still out riding bikes, playing ball.

"I've still got that pistol on you, DiPaulo," Carroway hissed.

"I figured that. My guess is that she told you when you came back to town. Yeah, I think that was when. See, I did a little checking. Sybil's parents left her about a cool million. A big chunk of that disappeared right after you were born. It cost her quite a bit to get that birth certificate and find out where you were. What a lucky break for her that it was right in the same town. Got to watch you grow up. You were probably in her class and never even knew that the drunk was old mommy dearest."

"My son in that pink monstrosity of a school. Never. I sent him to my old alma mater." Barton chuckled. "But, not bad. You got part of it right. Let's just say that Miss Gibney was a generous campaign donor. She didn't have to look for her son. It was all arranged beforehand. Her parents weren't using that money for anything worthwhile anyway."

The car turned into Evergreen Cemetery, the highest point in town. Perfect. At least, he'd be in the right place and he liked a view.

"So, I guess Sybil's mom and dad went to their reward a little early. Who's idea was that?"

Barton laughed again. "Oh, mine, of course. Sybil was a little unimaginative. I showed her the way in so many things."

"What's that supposed to mean?"

"You disappoint me, Agent DiPaulo. Alan is my real son. I took care of my mess. There were so many messes. I'm a very meticulous man and I think even you must know how much I hate having my schedule disturbed."

"Yeah, I do."

"Now you're wondering about Stone. That ridiculous fool. It made me laugh to think of his guilt all these years. In his own way, he was always so disgustingly honorable."

"Yeah, really disgusting."

The car stopped at the overlook, right next to the monument for an Indian girl who died in a train accident. From there you could see the whole town and he guessed it was probably the favorite parking spot of more than one teenaged couple. There wasn't going to be any parking that afternoon.

"Get out," Barton ordered.

The three of them got out. It really was a nice view. A guy could do worse for a final resting place.

"You never did answer my question."

"I suppose we could take the time to satisfy his curiosity, couldn't we, son?" The judge asked.

Carroway nodded. "Sure, whatever you say, Dad. What d'ya want to know? Make it quick. It's cold up here."

He was right. The wind had picked up and the grey sky threatened more snow. He glanced over the edge. It was a pretty sheer drop, but with any luck, he'd get out of it just fine. Just keep them talking till he knew the rest of the story, then make his move.

"When did Sybil tell you she was your mother? I can only assume he didn't tell you."

Barton piped up. "I never wanted him to know what a pathetic drudge his mother was."

"She was useful, though."

Barton smirked. "I have to agree with you."

"She came to my doorstep one day when I got back," Carroway told him. "She wanted to come meet me, my family. What an old fool. I wasn't about to introduce her to my wife. Can you imagine me parading her out in front of my kids? `Here kiddies, here's your granny'." He laughed. "Thank God no one but me was home. She was so nauseatingly desperate, like I was her last chance at something."

Barton shrugged his shoulders. "She was always that way. Clingy."

If he'd thought Carroway was disgusting before, this put him at a whole new level.

"Luckily my boy saw the potential."

"Yup, that big empty house, and so much desperation. It was just made for me. Close enough for me to hop through the backyards and be back at my own place before I was missed. Oh, the fun I had there."

"Yeah, I heard about some of the fun. I suppose there were others. I mean besides Debbie's girls and a that kid from Binghamton."

Carroway laughed. It seemed he'd gotten over the little beat-down. He was really warming up to the subject. "Not too many. Enough," he said coyly.

"And where was dear old mom while all this was going on?"

He snickered. "Where do you think? Passed out with her bottle of vodka. Never had the chance to keep one there, though. That was a treat. Too bad you had to mess that up."

"Is that why you spiked the old lady's booze?"

"Me. No. I really have no idea who killed her. But whoever did it, did the world a favor. And I could really use that thirty grand she saved up for me. Dear old mom...."

He didn't get out the next word. There were several loud reports. Carroway grabbed his chest, his mouth wide open and his eyes wide with surprise. His body hovered, suspended like that for several seconds before dropping in a heap.

Barton still had the gun pointed at his dead son.

"It saddens me," Barton shrugged, "but he'd become a liability, poor boy." Barton began to walk back to the car.

"So that's it. Don't you think I might say something about all of this?"

Barton turned and chuckled. A really funny guy. "Talk all you want. Your chief suspect was just executed with your own gun. A gun with your fingerprints all over it. Don't worry, I'll make sure it's found in an opportune spot. If there's one thing I've learned it's that you never kill a cop. The sentence is too long. Good-bye Agent DiPaulo."

The Olds took off down the winding road out of the cemetary.

"Think fast, DiPaulo."

It was the fastest way back to town. He half-crawled, half-fell down the cliff. When he finally landed on the road below, he could just see Barton's tail lights in the gathering dusk as the car came out of the cemetery's gates. He started running and didn't stop till he got to the gas station. Ten minutes later, a cab was dropping him off at Saint Patrick's, just down the street from Carroway's. He chatted with the driver about the mass. The cabbie wasn't Catholic, but liked Kennedy anyway. Go figure. Once the cab was gone, he pulled up his collar and walked down the street to Carroway's house. He pulled his car around the block, put on some gloves, then sneaked back to the doctor's garage. An amateur could've picked that lock. Two minutes later, he had what he wanted and was back in his car headed for the station. Two could play Barton's game.

He parked his car outside the station and went in.

Ford greeted him without looking up from his newspaper. "Hey, boss."

"I've gotta do some paperwork," he told his sergeant, "Don't let anybody in, okay?"

"Sure thing."

Once the office door closed, he quickly rifled the desk drawers looking for what he needed and shoved them in his coat pocket. He stopped to listen for a moment and decided no one was outside the door, then opened the window and slid out, dropping down next to the bushes. It was a good couple of miles back the cemetery, most of it uphill, and trying not to be seen.

By the time he got there, Carroway's body was starting to stiffen up. It was getting dark and he had to work fast. It was going to be a long night. He pulled out a pair of needle-nose pliers and began to go to work on the body. Lucky for him the cold had slowed down the blood flow, but it was getting too dark. He pulled a flashlight out of his pocket and put it in his mouth, trying his best to put sôme light where he needed it. The sky had turned purple, the light from the flashlight making the woods around him seem even more foreboding.

"C'mon," he ordered.

He dug around the open hole and finally hit metal. The other one came out easier. Making them disappear was easier. The Susquehanna was a big river with some heavy currents. When he got back to the office, he got in the same way he'd gotten out and Chuck was none the wiser. His sergeant was still reading the funnies. The only car anybody saw driving up into the cemetery that afternoon was the judge's, him and Carroway in the front seat. Probably twenty kids saw them. He'd been in the back, invisible to the world in the big coupe. He took his car and drove back down the dirt roads in Canawanna, stopping near a spot where the bushes thinned out. Making the slugs disappear would be easier than getting them out. After scraping them up with the pliers and wiping them down, he tossed them in the water. The Susquehanna was a big river with some heavy currents.

He could clean up messes too.

Step two wasn't so easy. Breaking into the Bureau of Motor Vehicles wasn't hard, but finding the paperwork was definitely tricky. It took a while, but by midnight the Fairlane was no longer registered to Alan Carroway. It was Judge Augustus Carroway Barton's and had been for years. There's nothing like an official record for evidence. The way he saw it as he filtered out into the crisp cold night was that Barton had helped his son all along. It was only fitting that he get whatever reward was coming to him.

CHAPTER ELEVEN

He put down the receiver. Johnson and the boys had hauled the judge in that morning. Seems they'd gotten an anonymous tip. He grabbed his coat. Time to tie up some loose ends.

"You're in charge, Ford."

"Yes, sir," the desk sergeant called after him.

The entrance to the Stone's house didn't let on about the ugliness that had been hidden behind those walls. Thanksgiving was nearly here. A gardener was raking leaves in the broad front lawn. Iron urns of orange and yellow mums lined the wide front steps leading up to the white-columned house. It looked like something out of "Gone with the Wind". The air of privilege felt heavy, like the grey sky that ominously pressed down.

He rang the bell and waited. There was a tapping of heels and Mildred Stone answered the door. She didn't look surprised.

"Well, come in," she said turning her back to him and leading the way into the dining room.

Cardboard boxes stood half full amongst piles of men's clothes.

"As you can see, I'm busy. What can I do for you?" she asked, not really paying attention to him. She was folding a tweed jacket. She held it for a minute, then put it in one of the boxes.

"You were there that night, weren't you?" he asked.

She hesitated, then picked up another jacket.

"I was, but I didn't poison her."

He nodded. "I know that. I just wanted to hear you admit what you did."

She took a cigarette out of an ivory case and lit it, then sat down on the green silk covered couch. She didn't invite him to sit.

"Do you know what it was like for me to watch her, to watch all of them, falling all over him? I couldn't go anyplace without women simpering all over him. It used to make me sick, the way they threw themselves at him. I knew he never wanted to marry me. After I got pregnant with Janie, he started sleeping in a separate room." She paused, then looked at him directly. "I know what you're thinking. You're thinking that I'm such a cold bitch you would've done the same thing." She laughed a little and drew on her cigarette again. "The funny thing is that everyone thought that Sybil was a bitch, too. But I knew what she was. She was weak. I usually ignored her, but then she came here one afternoon, right after Carroway came back. She was drunk, of course. I told her to leave but she laughed at me and then had the nerve to tell me about her son. That drunken fool threw it in my face that she'd had a son with my husband."

"Janie's husband."

She nodded and crushed out the cigarette. "I wanted to kill her. You see, Agent DiPaulo, I was never a beautiful woman, nor have I been especially liked, but I have standing and I wasn't about to let anyone take that from me."

"I don't suppose it meant anything to you that your daughter might've been hurt?"

"My daughter was the tramp that spread her legs for him. She brought on her own misery and could run away just like she did before if the truth came out. I was the one who would've suffered. I was the one with a reputation that would've been destroyed."

"So you stayed at the school after that meeting."

"I slipped away while Grant was being his charming self to all the bored housewives of Owego. I suspected Sybil would be in her classroom drinking. I went there and started talking to her. I was afraid she'd tell someone about her son, my son-in-law. I started telling her how useless and empty her life was, how she didn't have anything to live for. I kept pouring those drinks for her. At first I thought I'd just help her drink herself to death. I'm sure at this stage it wouldn't have taken much. And then I noticed those little first aid kits on the desks. Janie'd had to make one when she was little. I remember she'd wanted to buy extra iodine for her friends when they were making them, but the pharmacist wouldn't let her because it was poison. I knew then what I needed to do. I went around the room and gathered all the bottles while I was talking and put them in front of her."

He felt a chill run down his spine. "And you kept pushing."

She smiled. It was the coldest smile he'd ever seen. "She ran out of vodka and I began to open the tops of them. I kept telling her they were just as good as vodka, better. They were just sitting there in front of her, calling her. I told her I'd go get her another bottle. I went down the hall and waited and then I heard them, Grant and his whore. I saw them. I knew Sybil would know about them, too. I hated her for that. I hated her because her being alive and having that knowledge humiliated me. In order to not be humiliated, she needed to be dead. I went to Grant's office and found a bottle that he'd kept there, then I went back into her classroom and pushed and pushed and pushed until she picked up those bottles of iodine and drank them, every one of them. I gave her Grant's bottle to wash them down."

"You killed her."

"No, Agent DiPaulo, she killed herself."

Silence hung in the air of the perfect room.

He left her to the job of disposing of the last of her husband.

Carroway's report had arrived in the mail by the time he got back to the station. It said what he'd thought it would. Sybil had died of a broken neck. Because her liver was so damaged by alcohol, the iodine had affected it quickly. Delusional, in horrible pain and knowing she was dying, she'd gone down to the basement to find the only person she thought would help her.

Men like Grant Stone left a lot of wreckage in their wake.

He was packing up files when Struble came in. He was a little thinner from the hospital food, but other than that the same old guy with the goofy grin. Well, the same old guy with a pair of crutches.

"Well, the conquering hero," he greeted him. "How many channels ya got?"

Ford's voice came from the front desk. "Hey, Chief, can you fix my antenna?" That was followed by a lot of snickering.

Struble turned red and gave an embarrassed laugh. "Okay, comedians."

He held out his hand. "Good to have you back."

Struble laid the crutches down and hobbled to his seat. "Good to be back. That nearly drove me crazy, being laid up and all."

"The autopsy report came in. That teacher died of a broken neck. I'll finish the write up for you."

The smile faded from Struble's face. "Yeah, well, there's something I want to talk to you about."

He pulled up a chair. "Sure, sport. What is it?"

Struble got real serious. "I think you should stay," he blurted out.

Could've knocked him over. "What the hell are you talking about? You're the chief. You're right for this job. You can't just walk away a week before you get married. Patty'll kill you."

"Maybe, but I've been doing a lot of thinking over the past couple of weeks. I want to be chief, Nick, don't get me wrong, but I've got a lot to learn. I'm not stupid. If you hadn't been here to handle all this, I don't know what I would've done. I'd probably be screwing everything up. I need a chance to learn the job and I don't want to mess it up. When I think of that little girl..."

"Don't. It was dumb luck, that's all. I just stumbled onto it, and you would've done the same things I did."

"No, I wouldn't have. I mean it, Nick, I wouldn't have known where to start."

"You'll do just fine." He got up and patted Struble on the back. "I've gotta go. But thanks for thinking I could do it."

Struble stood up and put out his hand. "I mean it, if you change your mind."

"Thanks, chief. Be good to Patty."

He stepped out onto the stone steps. For once, there was some sun. It was cold. He probably ought to call his father and get things straightened out. He'd wait until Moriarty passed. It couldn't be long now. It was the least he could do for the guy.

He was packing the files into his trunk when he heard running feet.

"Hey, gonna leave without even a goodbye?"

Helen came running up to him. She still had her waitress uniform on. Must've just gotten off of work. He shut the trunk. "I'm not much of a friend," he said.

She grinned. "You're okay. She leaned against the hood of the car and held out a bag. "Some doughnuts."

"Cop food?"

"Yeah." she gave a little laugh, then sobered. "I heard about Jill."

"Me too."

"I'm kind of jealous. Rich husband, baby on the way, they're going to Hawaii for their honeymoon, did you know that?"

Her words were crashing around in his head like the jumbled pieces of glass in a dimestore kaleidoscope. "A baby?"

"Yeah. You didn't know? I guess I'm not supposed to know either, but I could tell.

The last time I was in to get my hair done, she was throwing up, then there's that little bump in her tummy. Jill's always been so thin, I noticed it right away. I figured something was going on when all of a sudden she was marrying Jeb like that...right after you left..."

Her words kept hammering at him until that was all he could hear.

"Yeah. Thanks, Helen. I've gotta get to the office." He said woodenly.

He started to leave, but she grabbed his arm and leaned up on her tiptoes, giving him a quick kiss on the cheek. "Take care of yourself."

"Yeah," he said, still in shock.

He went over it again and again as he drove to Binghamton. It was his kid. He knew it. His kid. He walked into the office in a daze, not noticing the man sitting at Moriarty's desk until he spoke.

"It's about time, DiPaulo," Ben Samuels greeted him. "Kind of late for an underling."

Then he noticed all the papers. There were papers all over the place, drawers open, cabinet doors askew. He was searching the office for the evidence Moriarty had on him.

"I'm taking Moriarty's spot for a while. No objections, I'm sure," Samuels told him, that sick, shit-eating smile on his face. "Want to make sure things are handled right while the guy's laid up."

He wanted to kick Samuels' teeth down his throat.

"Find what you're looking for?" he said.

Samuels looked down at the papers in his fist, the smile deepening, more taunting. "No, but I found something else. I thought it was kind of funny, that mafia fuck Cassetti getting off."

"Don't know what you're talking about."

Samuels laughed. "Yeah, well now I got you by the balls, goomba."

"Is that so."

Samuels laid the papers on top of the others. "Your buddy is a dead man, DiPaulo. When he goes, there ain't nothing that's gonna keep me from grinding you into the ground. You got a chance right now to do the right thing and tell me where Moriarty's little stash is. Maybe you'll save your career." He smirked. "Hey, maybe you won't end up in prison."

"Kiss my ass."

That wiped the smile off his face. "You stupid guinea son-of-a-bitch."

He pulled his badge out and put it on the desk. "You're right. I've got a chance to do the right thing."

He left to the sounds of Samuels trashing the office.

He got in his car and headed west towards Owego.

Made in the USA
Charleston, SC
27 November 2015